# Not Even Silence Stayed Empty

## The House We Are Building

Eleni Kapatou

Paperback: 978-1-968667-31-3
eBook: 978-1-968667-32-0
Library of Congress Control Number: 2025914982



This is a work of fiction.

Ordering Information:

Prime Seven Media
518 Landmann St.
Tomah City, WI 54660

Printed in the United States of America

# Table of Contents

# Angel Under the Rain: The House We Are Building

The rain fell the night Elara gave birth to Anny and Camille. Not gently—violently, with wind and memory and something else behind it. Something like warning. Or prophecy.

She had bled too much. And still, she had held on.

Anny was born first, fierce and tangled. Camille followed—quieter, smaller, blinking like he'd seen the world before.

Elara spent eight days in the hospital. She walked again after twenty-one. But her body was never quite the same—and neither was her heart.

She remembered her own birth. Not in detail, but in shape. In story. Her father—a navy captain—had nearly died the night she came into the world. Stabbed outside their home after a fight that had nothing to do with him. While her mother pushed life into being, her father's was slipping away.

She grew up loving a man who was often gone but never absent. A man who said, "You are not alone, mija," and meant it. A man who survived for her.

She missed him. Even now, even after years and oceans.

She wrote his story for her children, so they would know the man whose hands had planted her.

But more than anything, she wanted them to know her.

Not just the mother who cooked and painted and kissed their hair. The woman who ran. The girl who dreamed. The storm she had walked through.

Anny was the first to ask.

"Where were you born, Maman?"

So she told them. Slowly, in pieces. In poems. In paintings. In truths too heavy to speak all at once.

And the children—Anny, Camille, Aris, Alexander—each carried those truths in their own way.

Anny painted them, framing her mother's pain in light and gold. Camille painted the walls of the attic with family memory. Aris wrote letters in small, careful handwriting, whispering in a language Elara had left behind. Alexander set her silence to music.

And Nan—their father—wrote one letter.

"I stayed because love made me brave."

They built a room in their home. Not for guests. For them. For her. For truth.

They called it The House We Are Building, the Future.

And sometimes Elara stood in the doorway, watching her children create the future with the past she once feared would destroy her.

She had once stood in the rain, wings of memory behind her, refusing to break.

Now, her children stood in her light.
And the house held them all.

The angel. The rain.

The love that stayed.


The End.

*"Dedication" handwriting*

**"For You, When I Am Quiet or Absent"**
by Elara

*When the house is still*
*and you hear nothing but the soft breath of sleep,*
*know that I am still here—*
*folded into the silence*
*like light behind a closed door.*

*I did not come this far*
*to tell you how to live.*
*I came this far*
*to show you that you could.*
*I came this far to tell you that you are not alone—like my father*
*once told me.*
*I came this far to tell you how much I love you.*

*You, who are made of my softer hours*
*and my louder storms—*
*carry only what you must.*
*Let the rest turn to wind.*

*Forgive the nights I was tired.*
*Forgive the time I was absent.*
*Forgive your father.*
*Forgive us if it's not easy.*
*Forgive the truths I held too close.*
*I was learning how to be soft and brave*
*at the same time.*

*If I am not near—*
*if my voice feels far—*
*look to the sea.*
*Look to the rain.*
*Look to each other.*

*You are not my echo.*
*You are my answer.*

*And when the world begins to feel too loud,*
*place your hand over your heart,*
*and listen.*

*That rhythm?*

*That's me.*
*Still choosing you.*
*Always choosing you.*
*Always loving you.*

## CHAPTER ONE

# Shadows at Her Birth

The night she was born, blood painted the sidewalk outside their home.

Inside, the cries of a newborn girl mingled with the shouts of panic and sirens. Her mother clutched her tightly, unaware that just beyond their front door, the child's father lay gasping, a knife wound burning in his side and betrayal etched across his face.

It wasn't a stranger who had done this. It was someone from the neighborhood—someone he knew.

Earlier that day, there had been shouting. Two women. Two mothers. Old rivals with new resentments. What started as words over a fence turned into threats. And while no one believed the fight would go further than bruised pride and shouted insults, someone had taken it personally.

The attack came swiftly. He had stepped outside to smoke, to breathe, to calm his nerves after the chaotic birth. That's when he was jumped. The knife found his side, slicing through muscle and bone. And the last thing he saw before the world went black was the glint of cold eyes in a familiar face.

The baby's name was Elara. Her life began in the shadow of violence. But she would grow—strong, silent, and driven. What none of them knew then was that the attack was only the beginning.

Because secrets don't stay buried, and some rivalries never end.

## CHAPTER TWO

# Marisol
## (the mother of the attacker)

Marisol hadn't meant for blood to spill.

She just wanted to be heard—wanted to put that woman in her place. For too long, she'd watched Selene with her polished shoes and soft laugh, parading around like she was better than the rest of them. Acting like her baby's arrival was some kind of miracle when all it did was stir up dust in a neighborhood that had been quiet too long.

She remembered the heat of that afternoon. The argument had begun over something petty—trash bags left in the wrong spot, maybe a dog barking too late at night. But it was never really about that. It was about old slights, old wounds. The way Selene had humiliated her years ago at the school board meeting. The way their sons used to be friends—until they weren't.

Marisol didn't raise her voice much these days, but when she did, it cracked like a whip. That day, she let loose years of resentment. But when Selene threw back that insult—about her boy being "just like his father"—Marisol saw red.

That night, she couldn't sleep. Her son, Nico, hadn't come home yet. He was always temperamental, always too quick to take on her battles like they were his. But she never thought—

When the knock came just after midnight, her chest tightened. Not from fear. From knowing.

And when they told her what he'd done, that her boy had been the one to leave Selene's ( Elara's mother) man bleeding on the concrete, her knees buckled—not just from the horror, but from guilt.

She'd lit the match.

And now, the fire was spreading.

## CHAPTER THREE

# Nico
## (the attacker)

He hadn't planned to kill him.

Nico sat on the edge of the rusted rooftop behind Dallow Street, staring down at the alley where rats scurried and the streetlamp flickered like it was nervous. His hands still shook. He told himself it was the adrenaline. The fear. But deep down, he knew better.

It was the shame.

The knife hadn't felt like a weapon in his hand—it had felt like justice. That's how it started, anyway. He saw Selene's man come out of the house, relaxed, cigarette dangling from his lip like he had nothing to worry about. Like he didn't know the war that had been brewing on both sides of that picket fence for years.

Nico's mother had cried when she thought he couldn't hear. Always after fights with Selene. Always after pretending to be strong.

He hated that sound. More than anything.

So he followed the man. Confronted him. Words turned to shoves. A flash of metal. The feel of it sliding in. Warmth on his hand.

And the terrible silence afterward.

He hadn't run out of fear. He ran because in that moment, he had felt power. Not for himself, but for his mother. For the years she had swallowed her pride while people like Selene stood taller by tearing her down.

But now, sitting in the dark with blood under his fingernails, that power felt hollow.

He didn't know if the man would live. He didn't know if he wanted him to.

All he knew was this: that night changed everything. And once you cross a line like that, you can't go back.

Not ever.

CHAPTER FOUR

# Selene
## (the mother of the newborn and partner of the man who was stabbed)

She hadn't even held her daughter yet when the nurse burst into the delivery room with blood on her shoes.

Selene had seen panic before—she'd grown up with it—but never like this. Her body still trembled from the birth, still ached in places she hadn't known could ache. And now they were telling her that Miguel ( the father), the man who had whispered strength into her through every contraction, the man who left the room only to breathe, was lying in the street with a knife in his gut.

She barely remembered screaming.

The hours after blurred into shadows and sirens. The baby, Elara, was taken from her arms and handed back. Miguel was taken from her side and left in the hands of surgeons. Her world split down the middle—half in a hospital bed, half in an emergency room across the building.

No one would tell her much at first. Just that it was bad. That he might not make it.

She knew who did it before anyone said a word.

Not Nico himself—no, that part was a sick twist—but she knew where the hate came from. Marisol. That bitter woman with a sharp tongue and a gaze that cut deeper than any blade. She'd felt it for years. The tension. The jealousy. The quiet war on their block.

Selene had tried to rise above it. She had turned her cheek, again and again, pretending pride didn't matter. But pride was all they had in this neighborhood. Respect was currency. And Marisol had spent hers poisoning her own son.

Now Selene sat beside her newborn daughter in a room that smelled like bleach and betrayal, and something inside her hardened.

This wasn't over.

If Miguel survived, they would never come back to this street again. And if he didn't... she would never forgive. Not Marisol. Not Nico. Not herself for not seeing this coming.

Elara whimpered in her sleep.

Selene leaned down, brushing her lips over her daughter's soft head, and whispered a promise.

"Whatever comes, I will protect you. No matter what I have to do."

**Subject: Novel Chapter 5**

Let's continue in the present, still in the hours after the stabbing—but this time we shift focus to Miguel, the father, as he hovers between life and death. This chapter 5 dives into memory and the razor-thin space between holding on and letting go.

CHAPTER FIVE

# Miguel
### (the father)

There was a voice in the dark. Distant. Calling his name like it was the last word in the world.

Miguel drifted.

He wasn't sure if he was dreaming or dying. Pain had become distant, like a sound muffled under water. Somewhere, someone had their hands inside him—stitching, cutting, saving. Maybe. He didn't know.

What he did know was Selene's laugh. And he heard it now, echoing through some half-remembered summer. She was younger, barefoot, standing on the hood of his car, yelling at the stars. Back when they still believed that getting out of the neighborhood was just a matter of time and guts.

He tried to speak—to tell her he was still here—but his throat was sand.

Another memory rose. Holding Selene's hand as she pushed, sweat pouring down her face, fury in her eyes. He had never loved her more than in that moment. That moment, when she brought their daughter into the world with nothing but fire and will.

Elara.

His girl.

He hadn't even had time to see her properly.

And now, this.

There was something heavier than pain pressing down on him. Regret. He had gone outside for a break. Just five minutes. He didn't expect to be followed. Didn't see the kid coming. When the blade hit, it wasn't the pain that stunned him—it was the eyes. Nico's eyes. Wild, but not empty. Full of something worse than hate: belief. Like he thought he was doing the right thing.

That was the part that haunted him as the darkness came and went.

Not that he might die—but that a boy from the neighborhood, someone he'd once thrown a football to in the street, could be turned into a weapon by nothing more than words and poison.

If he made it out of this, he wouldn't just be fighting for his daughter. He'd be fighting for the kind of world she deserved to grow up in.

But first... he had to survive the night.

## CHAPTER SIX

# Selene
## (the mother of newborn child)

The clock on the wall didn't move.

Selene sat in a hard plastic chair outside the operating room, her newborn daughter wrapped against her chest like armor. The nurse had offered to take Elara back to the nursery, but Selene refused. She wouldn't be separated again—not from her baby, not from Miguel, her husband.

A doctor finally emerged. Young. Pale. Not nearly old enough to be carrying someone's life in his hands. His eyes said more than his mouth ever could.

"He made it through the surgery," he began, voice low, calm, rehearsed. "But he lost a lot of blood. He's stable, but not out of danger."

Selene nodded, lips pressed into a line. She wouldn't cry—not here, not in front of this stranger. Not with Elara watching.

"Can I see him?"

The doctor hesitated, then nodded once. "Just for a minute."

Inside the ICU, Miguel looked small. Smaller than the man who filled their home with music, who fixed the kitchen sink with nothing but a spoon and determination, who once held her up when her world fell apart after her father died.

Selene stepped to the bed, her free hand finding his. Cold. But there.

"I'm here," she whispered. "She's okay. We're okay."

Elara shifted in her arms, letting out a soft squeak. It broke something in Selene. Not into tears—into steel. Into resolve.

This wasn't just a feud anymore. It wasn't two women trading insults over fences.

This was war.

Marisol's son had tried to kill her partner. Had come to her doorstep with a blade. And now Marisol would face the cost. No more silence. No more walking away.

Selene leaned close to Miguel's ear. "You get better," she whispered, fierce. "But no matter what happens, I'll handle it."

She meant every word.

Because now, Selene wasn't just a mother. She was a guardian. A woman wronged. And she would burn down the lie of peace in that neighborhood if that's what it took to protect her child.

## CHAPTER SEVEN

# Marisol
## (the mother of the killer)

Marisol hadn't slept.

The neighborhood was silent, but her house was loud with ghosts—footsteps she imagined, voices she couldn't forget. Her son's voice, trembling the night he came home, eyes wide, hands shaking. "I didn't mean to, Ma. He pushed me. I didn't—"

She'd told him to run.

Not out of guilt. Out of fear. For him. For what would come next. Because deep down, she knew what she had done. Not with a weapon, not with her hands—but with her mouth. With years of bitterness fed to Nico like cold meals.

Now the police had been by. Brief questions. Calm tones that made her skin crawl. They weren't done. They would be back, and next time, they wouldn't ask. They'd take.

She sat at the kitchen table, staring at the photo of her husband. Dead ten years. A man who had started fights just to prove he was still the biggest shadow in the room. Nico had too much of him in him. And maybe too much of her, too.

She looked out the window. Across the street, Selene's house was quiet. Lights on in only one room. The baby's room, maybe. Or the hospital, she didn't know. Didn't want to know. Every time she tried to summon anger at Selene, it came back like a boomerang—sharp and aimed at her own chest.

How had it come to this?

She told herself she was protecting her family. But somewhere between the words and the wounds, she had become a threat to it.

And now she had a choice to make.

Stay silent, and lose her son to prison—or speak, and finally admit that she had been wrong. About Selene. About pride. About all of it.

For the first time in years, Marisol whispered a prayer. Not for herself. For the child across the street, born into a storm. And for the boy upstairs, who still thought he was saving her.

**Subject: Novel Chapter 8**

Here comes the moment both women knew was inevitable: the confrontation. It's quiet. It's daytime. But it carries the weight of years—and the sharp edge of everything they've lost and everything they're still willing to fight for.

CHAPTER EIGHT

# The Fence Between Them

Selene stood in her yard, the morning sun sharp behind her. The baby monitor was clipped to her hip, a quiet white hum whispering from it. Elara slept inside—safe, for now.

She didn't plan to go to Marisol's door ( the mother's attacker). She didn't need to. She knew Marisol would be watching. And sure enough, the screen door creaked open within seconds.

Marisol stepped out slow, like walking into a war she didn't want to fight.

They faced each other over the fence—the same one that had once held clotheslines and shared laughter. Before the men. Before the sons. Before their pride grew sharper than their love of peace.

Neither spoke.

Selene's voice was the first to break the silence, low and measured. "Your boy almost made my daughter an orphan."

Marisol flinched. "I know."

"You know?" Selene stepped closer to the fence. "You lit this fire, Marisol. And don't tell me you didn't know what you were doing. You've been aiming poison at my family for years. Nico just finally pulled the trigger."

"I didn't want this."

"But you didn't stop it, either."

Marisol's jaw clenched. Her voice cracked, softer than Selene expected. "He's still my son."

"And Miguel is still fighting for his life."

A pause.

Then: "Are you going to the police?" Marisol asked.

"I already did."

Silence again. Thick as cement. Behind Selene, a baby stirred over the monitor. Behind Marisol, a curtain moved upstairs.

Selene leaned in close, lowering her voice to a blade. "He's a child. But if he comes near mine again, I don't care whose blood I have to spill."

Marisol's eyes darkened. "Is that a threat?"

"No," Selene said. "It's a mother's promise."

She turned and walked away, not waiting for a response.

Because there was nothing left to say. The next move wasn't about words. It was about what came when justice didn't look like handcuffs—but like survival.

## CHAPTER NINE

# Nico
## (the attacker)

They always said silence was heavy. But this—this was louder than anything Nico had ever heard.

He sat on the edge of his bed, phone still glowing in his hand. His cousin had texted him just three words:

She went in.

Selene. The woman whose eyes he couldn't forget. The woman whose scream had echoed in his head ever since he'd run into the night with blood on his hands.

He already knew what it meant. The cops were coming. It was no longer a matter of if. It was when.

His heart thudded like a fist on a door. He stood, pacing his room, palms slick. The knife—the stupid, rusted thing he never should've carried—was gone. Dumped in the river. Didn't matter. They'd find him. Someone always talked.

He didn't blame her. Not really. Not even a little.

That's what made it worse.

He remembered the look on her face as she stood over Miguel ( Elara's father) in the hospital. He'd snuck in. Just once. From the hallway, hidden behind a curtain. The machines beeped slow and steady. Miguel looked pale, hollow. Like Nico had punched a hole in a man who didn't deserve it.

And maybe he had.

His mother told him it was an accident. Told him to keep quiet. Said the world would crush him if he let it in.

But he had let it in.

Every time he closed his eyes, he saw Miguel falling. Saw Selene's eyes. Heard the baby's cry through the open door.

He thought of turning himself in. Just walking to the station, saying I did it. It was me. Don't blame her. Don't blame my mom. It was me.

But then what?

He'd be just another angry kid in handcuffs. Just another case file.

So instead, he opened the window. Climbed out. And ran. Not away.

Just... somewhere.

Somewhere he could breathe before the sky closed in.

**Subject: Novel Chapter 10**

Here comes the moment that has been building since the blade hit the pavement: the police arrive at Marisol's house. Truth, fear, and the collapse of a mother's last illusion.

CHAPTER TEN

# Blue Lights

They didn't knock like neighbors.

It was early—barely light out—when the pounding came. Not fists. Not friendly. The sound of law. Hard, cold, practiced.

Marisol was already awake, sitting at the kitchen table with a cup of coffee she hadn't touched. She knew before she opened the door. She had known since the moment she saw Selene cross the street days earlier, her jaw set like stone.

She opened the door slowly. No words.

Two officers. One male. One female. No guns drawn. No yelling. But they didn't need to.

"Marisol Vega?" the woman asked, already checking a clipboard she didn't need to look at. "We have a warrant to search the premises. We're also looking for your son. Is he home?"

Marisol didn't answer.

Behind her, the house was silent. Nico's room: door closed. She hadn't checked this morning. Hadn't dared.

"Ma'am?"

She stepped aside.

The officers entered, methodical. Polite. Efficient. But their presence filled the space like smoke. One of them moved upstairs. She heard the creak of Nico's door, the shuffle of drawers being opened.

"He's not here," the other officer said after a minute.

Marisol didn't flinch.

She hadn't seen Nico since the night he left through the window. She told herself he just needed time. That he'd come home. That if she kept the porch light on, he'd see it from wherever he was.

But now the light felt like a lie.

The female officer turned to her gently. "If he contacts you, you need to let us know. This won't go away. And the longer he runs, the harder it gets."

Marisol nodded. Not because she agreed. But because she had nothing left to say.

As they left, she stood alone in the doorway, watching the blue lights fade down the block. People were peeking out of blinds. The neighborhood always watched. Always whispered.

She had been the firestarter.

And now the whole street was burning.

**Subject: Novel Chapter 11**

Let's go intimate. We return to Selene (Elara's morher), just after she learns the police came up empty. She thought justice was coming. Now she realizes—sometimes justice runs.

# CHAPTER ELEVEN

# Smoke

Selene, Elara's mother sat in the nursery, the soft whir of the mobile above Elara's crib the only sound in the room. It spun slowly—clouds and stars and a sun with a smiling face. A gift from Miguel before the baby came. Before the knife. Before everything cracked.

She got the call an hour ago.

The police had searched Marisol's house. Nico was gone. No trace. No confession. No cuffs.

Gone.

Selene didn't scream. Didn't cry.

She just... sat. Elara's tiny hand curled around her finger like a promise, warm and fragile and real.

Miguel, the father was still in the hospital. Alive. Healing, slowly. But sleeping more than speaking. He didn't know yet that the boy who nearly killed him had vanished into the night like a ghost.

She couldn't tell him. Not yet.

Because beneath her anger, beneath the fear, beneath the mother-lion instinct clawing at her chest, something else was growing.

A thought.

If the system couldn't find Nico... maybe she could.

Selene had lived in this neighborhood her whole life. She knew its shadows. Its secrets. Its alleys and hideouts and uncles who owed her favors. She knew where kids ran when they needed to disappear.

And she knew one truth better than most: sometimes justice wasn't delivered. Sometimes, you had to take it.

She leaned down and kissed Elara's head. "I'll be back soon," she whispered.

Then she stood, slid on her coat, and tucked something into her pocket. Not a weapon. Not yet.

But something heavier.

Intent.

**Subject: Novel Chapter 12**

Now we follow Nico, alone, hunted not just by the law—but by the woman whose life he nearly destroyed. This chapter is quiet, raw, and filled with the tension of a boy running out of places to hide.

CHAPTER TWELVE

# Hiding Places

Nico, the attacker had been gone three nights.

He didn't count them. Just knew by the ache in his back from sleeping on concrete, by how many bags of chips and gas station burritos he had left. He was holed up in the back of an abandoned auto shop two blocks from the freeway, a place he used to tag with his friends. No one came here anymore.

The windows were boarded. The air stank of rust and oil. But it was quiet. No cops. No questions. Just silence and the occasional rat.

He kept the lights off. His phone was dead—tossed into a sewer grate the night he ran. It buzzed with guilt before it went dark. Calls from his mom. Messages from friends. One from an unknown number he knew was her.

Selene.

He couldn't stop thinking about her face. Not the day of the stabbing—after. The day she looked him dead in the eyes through her window. There was no screaming. No crying. Just cold. Focused. Like she had crossed some invisible line and wasn't turning back.

And she knew where to look.

Nico had seen her growing up—sharp, proud, unbreakable. His mom called her fake. But he remembered a day when Selene pulled his little sister out of traffic and handed her back, just a soft hand on the shoulder and a "watch the street, baby." Like it was nothing. Like she protected kids, even ones that weren't hers.

Now she was coming. He could feel it.

He sat on the floor, knees pulled to his chest, staring at a cracked mirror leaning against the wall. His face looked older now. Harder. Not grown. Just... worn down by a weight he didn't know how to carry.

He didn't want to be the villain in this story. He didn't even want to be in it anymore.

But stories don't let you go once you've drawn blood.

And somewhere out there, he knew, Selene was walking through the dark—closer every hour.

## CHAPTER THIRTEEN

# The Choice

It was Lupe from down the street who told her.

Marisol hadn't asked. She hadn't gone looking. But word traveled in their neighborhood like smoke—silent and fast. Over a shared cigarette and a long pause, Lupe had said, "He's in the old McAllen shop. Near the overpass."

Just like that.

Marisol didn't thank her. Didn't move. Just stared down at her coffee like she could see the end of the story in the cream swirl.

She waited until nightfall.

Then she drove without headlights through the back alleys, her car tires crunching slow over broken glass and gravel. When she parked behind the old auto shop, her hands wouldn't stop shaking. Not from fear—but from memory. She used to ride past this place on the handlebars of Nico's father's bike, laughing like the world was wide open.

Now it felt like it was closing in.

She found him behind a busted lift, curled up in a nest of rags and cardboard like a stray. He didn't speak when she stepped into the dim, rust-smelling gloom. Just looked at her, eyes hollow and tired.

"Mijo," she said softly. "You look like a ghost."

He sat up slowly. "I thought you wouldn't come."

"I shouldn't have."

Silence.

She knelt beside him, brushing hair from his face. He looked like a boy again in that moment—her boy. But the dried blood on his sleeve and the weight in his eyes reminded her he wasn't innocent anymore.

"I can't keep you safe," she said. "Not from this."

"I know."

"You have to go," she whispered. "Turn yourself in. Let the lawyers fight. Maybe... maybe if you speak, if you own it, they'll show mercy."

He shook his head. "You saw her face, Ma. Selene's not giving mercy. She's coming."

Marisol closed her eyes. Her heart ached in a way that made breathing feel wrong. She wanted to run with him, like in the old stories—mother and son against the world.

But this wasn't a story anymore.

It was real. And the damage was done.

"I raised you to fight," she said. "But I didn't raise you to run."

She pulled out a burner phone. Slid it across the floor to him. "Call them. Before she finds you first."

Then she stood and walked to the door.

Before stepping out, she said one last thing. "I'll always love you. But love can't fix this."

And then she left.

**Subject: Novel Chapter 14**

This chapter is quiet. No sirens. No chase. Just a boy finally stepping out of the shadow he helped cast. Nico calls in—and begins the long road toward owning what he did.

## CHAPTER FOURTEEN

# Surrender

The phone felt heavier than it should have. Like it knew what was coming.

Nico stared at it for a long time after his mother left. Her words still echoed in the empty shop: I didn't raise you to run. She had looked so tired when she said it. Like she'd aged ten years in ten minutes.

He pressed the button.

One ring.

Two.

"911. What's your emergency?"

His voice was barely there. "I—I need to turn myself in."

A pause.

"Are you in danger?"

"No. Not anymore."

The dispatcher's voice softened slightly. "What's your name, son?"

He swallowed. "Nico Vega."

Another pause. Longer. His name was already in the system. They knew.

"Where are you right now, Nico?"

He gave them the address. Told them he'd wait. No weapon. No resistance.

Then he ended the call. Sat down on the cracked tile floor. He didn't cry. Didn't pace.

He waited.

The silence stretched so long it felt like a blanket—thick, suffocating, but somehow comforting. For the first time in days, he wasn't running. For the first time, he was choosing to stop.

When the sirens finally came, they were soft. No blaring, no flashing chaos. Just the low hum of something inevitable.

He walked out with his hands raised.

Two officers cuffed him. One of them asked if he was hungry. He nodded, once. They didn't shove him. Didn't speak to him like he was trash. That surprised him.

As the cruiser pulled away, he looked back at the old auto shop.

And let it go.

## CHAPTER FIFTEEN

# Waking

The first thing Miguel felt was the light.

Not pain. Not voices. Just light—pale and sharp against his eyelids, like morning through a cracked window. Then came the sounds. A beeping monitor. A soft mechanical hiss. A chair creaking beside him.

He turned his head, slow as stone, and saw Selene asleep next to the bed, one hand curled near his. Her other hand held a baby sock. Elara's.

He tried to speak. Nothing came.

Selene, the mother stirred, blinked—and when her eyes landed on his, the world stopped moving.

"Miguel," she whispered.

He managed the smallest nod.

Tears sprang to her eyes before she could stop them, but she didn't cry—not fully. She leaned in, kissed his forehead, then exhaled like she'd been holding her breath for years.

"You're here," she said. "You stayed."

He wanted to ask about his baby Elara. About what happened. But Selene seemed to understand the question without a word.

"She's safe. We're okay."

She hesitated then, her face hardening slightly. "Nico turned himself in last night. The police have him."

Miguel closed his eyes.

He didn't feel relief. Not exactly. More like... weight. A stone finally placed where it belonged.

Selene brushed her fingers through his hair. "He called himself in, Miguel. No chase. No violence. I think... maybe he realized what he did."

He opened his eyes again. Looked at her.

"You didn't go after him?" he whispered, voice cracked.

Her silence told him everything.

"I would've," she said. "I almost did."

He looked at her hand—bruised from gripping things too hard. "Thank you."

She nodded, then pulled out a photo from her pocket. Elara, sleeping, one fist clenched beside her cheek like a little fighter.

Miguel stared at it a long time.

"She's stronger than both of us," he murmured.

Selene smiled. "She has to be."

They sat in silence then. No monitors, no doctors, no sirens. Just the beginning of what came next.

**Subject: Novel Chapter 16**

Let's walk with Elara as she grows—under the shadow of what happened, but also through her own path. This chapter shifts the focus to her as an older child, just beginning to understand the world she was born into.

## CHAPTER SIXTEEN

# The Girl Who Was Born in a Storm

Elara was ten the first time she asked about the scar.

Not hers—her father's.

They were planting tomatoes in the backyard, dirt under her nails, sun on her back. Miguel, her father knelt beside her, laughing as she asked whether tomato vines had feelings. Then her eyes fell on the thin, pale line that cut across his ribs like a cruel whisper.

"What happened there?" she asked.

Miguel paused, his hand frozen in the soil.

Selene, her mother looked up from the porch, where she was folding laundry. For a moment, time held its breath.

He wiped his hands, sat beside her in the dirt.

"I got hurt," he said simply. "Before you were old enough to remember."

"By who?"

His eyes met Selene's. She gave a small nod.

"By a boy who made a very bad choice," Miguel said. "He didn't know how to deal with his anger, and he listened to people who were hurting, too."

Elara frowned. "Did you forgive him?"

Miguel hesitated.

"I worked hard to," he said. "Sometimes I do. Some days, I don't. Forgiveness is... like a muscle. You have to keep using it, or it gets weak."

She didn't speak for a while. Just pressed a tomato seed deep into the soil.

"Mom says I was born the night you got hurt."

"You were," he said. "You saved me."

She turned to him then, serious in that way only kids could be. "Then that means I'm strong, right?"

Miguel smiled.

"Stronger than anyone I know."

---

Elara grew tall. Grew curious. Grew watchful.

The other kids at school sometimes whispered about her family. About "what happened." Some got the story wrong—most never knew the truth.

Elara never corrected them. But she watched. She listened. She learned who told the truth and who hid behind anger.

By thirteen, she could out-argue anyone in class.

By fifteen, she started volunteering at the legal aid clinic in town, helping kids who reminded her of someone. Of Nico, the attacker. Of herself.

She didn't know exactly what she wanted to become. A lawyer? A writer? A social worker?

But she did know this: no one would ever be hurt again on her watch. Not without someone standing in the way.

She was born into a storm. But she was not made of its wreckage.

She was made of the "fire" that came after.

**Subject: Novel Chapter 17**

Let's continue with Elara—now a teenager, standing at the edge of adulthood. The past has shaped her, but now she begins to confront it on her own terms.

## CHAPTER SEVENTEEN

# The Echo

Elara was seventeen the first time she saw Nico Vega.

She didn't recognize him at first.

It was at a community youth panel downtown—something her civics teacher had begged her to attend. Local mentors. Talks about second chances, cycles of violence, prison reform. She had gone mostly for extra credit.

The man onstage was quiet. Didn't speak much. Just sat off to the side in a plain black shirt and jeans, arms folded, eyes down. He looked... ordinary. Tired. Young, but older than he should've been.

The moderator introduced him halfway through. "This is Nico Vega— he works at Westside Auto and volunteers with reentry programs. He spent three years in a juvenile facility and has since devoted his life to helping other young men stay out of the system."

Elara's breath caught.

Nico Vega.

That Nico.

Her mind blurred. Faces flashed—her mother's clenched jaw. Her father's scar. The stories no one ever told her, but that she pieced together over years like puzzle pieces hidden under floorboards.

She barely heard the rest of the discussion.

Afterward, people filtered out. She stood in the corner, unsure if she was furious or frozen. Her hands trembled, not from fear—but from weight. The weight of history.

He was gathering papers, about to leave.

She stepped into his path.

"Nico."

He stopped. Looked up. And the moment their eyes met, she knew.

He recognized her.

"Elara," he said quietly. Like the name itself asked for forgiveness.

Neither moved.

"You knew who I was," she said. "The whole time."

He nodded once. "I wasn't going to say anything."

"Why are you here?" she asked. "Why now?"

His voice was steady, but soft. "Because I thought if I did something good with my life... maybe I wouldn't just be the boy who ruined yours."

Silence.

She studied him—looking for something, anything. Anger, guilt, lies. But all she saw was a man carrying a shadow. One he didn't want to hide from anymore.

"I don't forgive you," she said.

He nodded again.

"But I'm not going to run from you, either."

Then she turned and walked away.

Outside, the sky was gray. Not storming. Not clear. Just honest.

Elara didn't know what came next.

But she knew this: she had faced the past.

And she was still standing.

CHAPTER EIGHTEEN

# Glow

Elara had just turned twenty-five when she stood in front of the courtroom—not as a defendant, not as a victim, but as a lawyer.

Her first trial.

It wasn't a dramatic case—no headlines, no jury gasps. A juvenile assault hearing. A scared fifteen-year-old girl who threw a chair at a teacher after months of being bullied. The kind of case people roll their eyes at, unless they've lived a life where no one listens until something breaks.

Elara listened.

She stood in that courtroom with calm in her voice and a fire in her spine. She told the story behind the charges. Explained the pressure, the pain, the quiet rage of being unheard.

She won.

Not by shouting. But by telling the truth with the kind of strength that only comes from living it.

Afterward, she sat alone on the courthouse steps, feeling the weight and wonder of the moment. She had imagined this so many times. Not for glory—but for the kid in front of her who might now have a chance she almost never got.

Her phone buzzed.

A message from her mother.

> Proud of you, baby. You're making us whole.

She smiled. Miguel her father had called earlier too, voice hoarse with emotion. He still limped, still carried that scar—but he danced with Selene in the kitchen most nights now, laughing louder than ever.

Elara closed her eyes for a moment. Remembered the fire of her childhood. The blood. The fence. The silence. The way people used to look at her with pity or curiosity.

They didn't anymore.

Now, when they looked at her, they saw purpose.

She was no longer the girl born into a storm.

She was the storm.
And the light that followed it.

## CHAPTER NINETEEN

# Home Soil
## (with painting and deeper emotion)

The house looked smaller, but the light inside it still pulled her in.

Elara stood at the gate with a store-bought pie in hand and something heavier in her chest. Her feet didn't want to move, even though this path had once been hers. She'd walked it barefoot in summer storms, tiptoed it home after late-night debates in high school, stomped it in fury when her mother said no to things she couldn't explain.

She breathed in.

And stepped forward.

The fence was new. Her mother's work—Elara could tell by the neat edges, the careful brush strokes of stain. Selene had always hated mess, but when it came to rebuilding the fence, she had left a small heart carved into the inside post. Elara ran her fingers over it.

She remembered carving hearts into corners when she was little.

And painting.

Inside, nothing had changed—and everything had.

The walls were filled with her old artwork. Watercolor skylines. Charcoal portraits of her parents. Small, messy canvases from when she was seven and obsessed with stars and fireflies. Her teenage years were heavier—abstract storms, harsh strokes of reds and blacks—but her mother had hung those too, never once hiding the darkness.

Selene her mother said it was all part of the story.

"You're back," Selene said from the kitchen doorway, a soft smile on her face. "We saved you a seat."

Elara placed the pie on the counter and wandered through the living room like a visitor in her own memory. Her eyes landed on a large canvas by the stairs—her favorite. She had painted it the summer she turned fifteen. It was just two hands reaching for each other across a chasm of color, like they were trying to hold on through fire.

She hadn't understood why she painted it back then.

She did now.

They ate together. They laughed. Her father teased her about law school and asked if she still painted. Selene swore the pie was store-bought but ate three slices anyway.

And then, when the light faded outside and the world softened, Elara slipped into the backyard alone.

The garden was new, but the soil was old. Familiar.

She held the seed packet in one hand, the memory in the other. The same earth that once soaked in her father's blood now cradled life. Color.

As she knelt to press the tomato seeds into the dirt, she felt a presence behind her.

Miguel joined her silently, as he always did when it mattered.

"I used to think nothing good would ever grow here again," he said, placing his hand gently on hers.

She didn't look at him. She was watching her fingers disappear into the soil, painting with dirt this time.

"And now?" she asked.

"Now I know," he said, voice thick, "you were always the thing growing."

She turned then. Not just to look at him—but to see him.

And to be seen.

The tears came freely. No hiding them. Not anymore.

He reached for her, pulled her into a quiet, full embrace. She let herself lean into it like she did when she was five and believed he could fix anything.

And then he said the words she didn't know she needed to hear.

"You are not alone, "mija"."

Her breath caught in her chest.

Behind them, Selene stood in the doorway, arms crossed, eyes shining.

The house was full of paintings—scars turned into color, memories turned into brushstrokes. But this moment... this was the first time in years they were painting something new.

Together.

**Subject: Novel Chapter 20**

let's bring this final chapter to life with vivid detail. We'll enrich the mural with symbolism, tie in Elara's secret love of songwriting, and show how her gifts ripple outward through others. This chapter celebrates creativity, community, and healing through shared art.

CHAPTER TWENTY

# The Wall
## (Expanded – The Mural and the Music)

The west wall of the Delano Street Rec Center was blank no longer.

Now, it breathed.

Elara stood before it, the last rays of afternoon light casting fire across her work. The mural towered above her, twenty feet wide and radiant with color, memory, and unspoken truths.

At the center of the piece, a massive hand rose from the ground—weathered, dark-skinned, cracked but steady. It was made of roots and veins and wounds—a symbol of all the hands that held her when she didn't know how to stand.

From the palm of the hand, trees grew. But not just any trees.

Children.

Painted as oak saplings and olive branches, each child's body curved and stretched like a stem reaching toward the sky—one in mid-laugh, one drawing with a stick in the dirt, another playing an invisible violin.

Among them, a girl with wild curls stood barefoot on the edge of the palm, holding a paintbrush like a sword.

Behind them, a skyline bloomed—buildings breaking open into petals and leaves. Chain-link fences unraveled into staves of music. Broken glass refracted light into color.

And down near the bottom, nestled into the roots, was a single, quiet scar—deliberate. Real. Uncovered.

Not erased.

Incorporated.

The mural wasn't just about survival.

It was about transformation.

But Elara hadn't stopped with paint.

In the months leading up to the project, she had quietly returned to something she'd abandoned for years: songwriting.

It started with poems. Fragments. Then melodies that haunted her in the quiet hours. She wrote at night, often curled up on her childhood bed, lyrics pouring out like breath after years of holding it in.

When she finished, she passed her songs to friends—musicians, singers, kids she had mentored. She told them, these aren't mine to keep.

And on the day she unveiled the mural, they came.

A small group of them—former students, a gospel duo, a street violinist—gathered in front of the wall with simple instruments: guitar, keyboard, a beatbox, and trembling courage.

And they sang.

The first song was called "We Grew Here"—a soft, aching anthem Elara had written after planting tomato seeds in her parents' garden. The chorus rose like a sunrise:

> We are not made of rubble /
We are not just what we lost /
We are roots, and bloom, and thunder /
We are worth the cost.

The crowd quieted as the music filled the space.

Parents held children tighter. A woman in the back wiped her eyes. Miguel stood with his hand over his heart. Selene closed her eyes and whispered the words as if they were a prayer.

And Elara?

She stood beside the mural, not in front of it. This wasn't about her.

It was about them.

Her community.

Her past.

Her future.

Nico Vega ( the attacker) stood at the edge of the crowd, arms crossed, head bowed—not asking for recognition. Just present. Listening.

As the final chords rang out, the mural seemed to glow under the fading sun. Not in color—in meaning.

It was more than a wall.

It was a wound made into wonder.

A home for those who didn't have one.

A canvas of resilience.

And Elara—artist, advocate, survivor, and song-giver—felt no need to speak.

The art spoke for her.

And it would keep speaking long after she was gone.

**Subject: Novel Chapter 21**

let's take Elara into a new chapter of life and love. She's built herself from fire and color. Now she meets someone who once knew her as a girl, and now sees the woman she's become. This chapter introduces Nan, her past-summer-school crush, now a man with secrets and a job that comes with shadows.

## CHAPTER TWENTY-ONE

# The One She Remembered

It was at a security conference in Manhattan, New York where Elara saw him again.

She wasn't even supposed to be there. She'd been invited last-minute to speak on a panel about restorative justice and art activism. When she arrived—badged, exhausted, coffee in hand—she wasn't looking for anything but the exit.

Until she saw him standing near the back of the room.

Tall. Still lean like she remembered, but the boyish edge was gone. He was sharper now. Structured. Dressed in a simple black suit with a discreet earpiece tucked behind one ear, scanning the crowd like a man used to not being seen.

He saw her instantly.

And smiled.

It hit her like a warm wind from another lifetime.

"Elara?" he said, crossing the room like no time had passed. "Tell me that's really you."

She laughed before she meant to. "Nan Malik. You still exist?"

"Barely," he said, and they hugged like two people who had once shared something brief, bright, and unfinished.

They'd met at a summer prep school in New York when she was sixteen. Her father had scraped together everything to send her, desperate to push her past the weight of the neighborhood. Nan had been the boy who quoted poetry at lunch and stole cookies from the staff lounge. They had kissed once. Only once.

And then never saw each other again.

Until now.

"I work in counterintelligence," he said quietly over dinner that evening, after her panel. "Can't say much more than that."

"You always did like secrets," she teased, sipping her wine.

"And you," he said, studying her face, "always had too much light to be hiding in anyone else's shadow."

The conversation flowed like they were catching up after a long dream. She told him about the mural. The music. Her parents. He told her about the work—traveling, quiet missions, watching people who never knew they were being seen.

When she asked why he stayed in that world, he said something that caught her breath.

"Because not everything broken gets the chance to rebuild. And I can't paint. But I can protect the people who do."

They walked through the city after dinner—her coat wrapped tightly around her, his shoulder brushing hers in that way that made her heartbeat start rearranging itself.

"Did you ever think we'd meet again?" she asked.

"No," he said. "But I never stopped hoping."

At her hotel, he didn't ask to come up. He didn't have to.

They stood at the door, quiet, the city humming beneath them.

He leaned in, slow. Gentle.

And kissed her like someone who had waited to get it right.

---

Subject: "Novel Chapter 22" The Capital
(Fully Expanded – Jazz, Memory, and the Long Night)

Let's deepen this chapter even more with a richly intimate moment after dinner—a sultry jazz bar, music low, memories stirred, and the quiet ache of connection years in the making. Here's the expanded Chapter Twenty-Two, now infused with atmosphere, longing, and the echo of a childhood kiss that never faded.

## CHAPTER TWENTY-TWO

# The Capital
## (Fully Expanded – Jazz, Memory, and the Long Night)

Washington was colder than Elara expected.

Not just the weather—but the pace, the posture, the way the city never fully exhaled. Everyone here moved like they were carrying things they couldn't speak about.

Nan blended in perfectly.

They arrived late on a Friday, both fresh off separate flights—his from a debriefing in London, hers from a youth mural summit in Chicago. It was their first real time away together. Not chance meetings. Not brief dinners in borrowed cities. Intentional time.

He didn't take her to an Airbnb or a chain hotel. He'd reserved a room at the Georgetown Inn, one of the oldest boutique hotels in the area, nestled among red-brick townhouses and gaslit sidewalks. The room had tall windows, heavy velvet curtains, a writing desk that looked like it belonged to a senator's grandmother, and a faint scent of cedar and worn books.

Elara loved it instantly.

"This is where I disappear when I need peace," he said, dropping his bag inside.

"You disappear a lot?" she asked, setting her sketchbook down on the desk.

He nodded. "More than I like."

She turned to him, eyes steady—her blue eyes catching the soft lamplight like water under a full moon.

"Then don't disappear from me."

He didn't promise anything. Nan never did. But he came to her, wrapped his arms around her waist, and said, "I won't if you don't."

His own blue eyes held a different kind of light—cooler, watchful, like the calm before a storm. But when he looked at her, it softened. Opened.

They matched in color. But hers were fire beneath ice.

His were sky behind walls.

---

After a long walk through the glowing streets of Georgetown and a lingering dinner at Martin's Tavern, Nan surprised her with one last stop.

"A place I want you to see," he said, guiding her down a narrow alley glowing with string lights.

The door was small and unmarked, just a bronze handle and a bouncer who seemed to know Nan on sight.

Inside, the air was low and warm—liquid velvet. A tiny, hidden jazz club with tables the size of dinner plates, all candlelit. A stage barely raised, where a trio played slow, aching blues like they were pouring secrets into the room.

They found a booth near the back. He ordered her a dark red wine. He drank bourbon neat.

They didn't talk much.

They didn't need to.

The music filled the space between them—lazy horns, honey vocals, drums like a heartbeat in the dark.

And then, somewhere between the second glass and the third song, he leaned in.

Slowly. Intentionally.

His lips found the soft place just beneath her ear.

The side of her neck.

And suddenly—

She was sixteen again.

Summer school in New York. Midnight curfew. Whispered jokes beneath dorm covers. And one kiss—just there—on her neck, so shy it had felt like breath more than touch.

It had haunted her for years.

Now, his kiss was firmer. Certain. But the feeling was the same: like the whole world had narrowed to a single point of heat and memory.

Elara closed her eyes.

Too many emotions rose in her chest—longing, disbelief, the ache of years lost and the thrill of something rediscovered. Her fingers gripped the edge of the table. She didn't know if she wanted to cry or kiss him back harder.

He whispered, "I never forgot that night."

"Neither did I," she breathed.

The night stretched long after that.

They stayed until the club dimmed its lights and the last saxophone note faded into silence. They walked back to the hotel slowly, brushing against each other like the world had gone quiet around them.

When they reached their room, she turned to him in the doorway, heart racing.

No words.

Just her hands at the collar of his shirt, and his gaze locked to hers— blue to blue, no hiding, no fear.

And in the quiet that followed, she let him all the way in.

Not just into her room.

Into her life.

---

Here is a sensual, emotionally charged scene between Elara and Nan, set in the quiet of their hotel room in Washington, D.C., after the jazz bar—the night is heavy with memory, desire, and trust.

---

The rain hadn't started yet, but the sky had softened. Outside their hotel window, the streetlights cast long, golden streaks across the wet stone of Georgetown. The jazz still echoed in Elara's ears—soft, smoky, slow. Nan had said almost nothing since they left the bar, but his hand had never left hers.

Now they were inside. The door shut. The silence was thick.

Elara stepped out of her heels and turned toward the window, her back to him. She could feel him watching her. Not just her body. Her breath. Her hesitations.

"Say something," she said quietly.

"I've been waiting for this moment my whole life," he answered.

She turned.

The space between them collapsed in a breath. Nan kissed her—harder than he meant to, softer than she expected. It wasn't rushed. It wasn't polite. It was full of all the years between the kiss on her neck as children and the ache that never fully left them.

His hands moved to her waist, holding her like he needed proof she was real. Her fingers slid into his hair. The air changed.

He pushed her against the wall.
Their mouths found each other again and again—sometimes slow, sometimes with urgency. Clothes slipped away, not in haste but in surrender.

There was no fear. No shame. Just the rhythm of trust.

He pulled her towards the bed, Elara lay back first, her hair fanned out against the white sheets, her eyes locked on his.
Nan leaned over her, tracing the side of her face with his thumb. "I never stopped looking for you."

"You didn't have to," she whispered. "I've been waiting for you to arrive."

When he entered her, it was like breathing after holding your breath for years. Her body welcomed him without question. Their movements were not polished or perfect—but they were real. Raw. Filled with knowing.

She arched into him, lips parted with every breath, every release of something held too long.

He held her face in both hands when she came undone beneath him, eyes wide, mouth silent, every inch of her trembling with memory and release. And when he followed—face buried in her neck—he exhaled her name like a promise.

———————————————————————————————————————

Later, when they lay tangled together, Elara pressed her palm over her belly—without thinking, just feeling.

Nan noticed but didn't ask.

Outside, the rain began to fall.

And inside that quiet, "something began:.

They wouldn't know it yet—not for weeks.
But that night, in the hush of a Georgetown hotel, two lives began, the twins.

And for the first time in years, Elara fell asleep in someone's arms— without having to keep one eye open.

**Subject: Novel Chapter 23**

Let's continue with Elara painting Nan's portrait—a deeply personal act that reveals how she sees him, not just as a man of shadows, but as someone who has become part of her light. This chapter blends intimacy with artistic vulnerability and becomes a moment of quiet trust between them.

## CHAPTER TWENTY-THREE

# The Portrait

The idea came to her quietly—like most important things did.

It was the morning after they returned from Washington. Elara stood barefoot in her studio, the soft hum of rain against the windows, her brush hovering above a blank canvas. The room smelled of oil paint and jasmine tea. Light filtered through the high windows like silk.

She wasn't sure when she decided it, but it had been stirring since Georgetown.

She would paint him.

Not just his face. Not a snapshot. But Nan—as she saw him.

At first, she sketched from memory. The line of his jaw. The shadow beneath his lower lip when he was thinking. The quiet coil of his shoulders when he stood still too long, listening for something he couldn't name. But it wasn't enough.

She needed him there.

"Come sit," she told him the following Saturday.

He raised an eyebrow. "You're painting me?"

"You trust me?"

He gave a quiet smile. "Always."

---

Nan sat in the middle of the studio, perched on an old wooden stool. He wore a simple black button-up and charcoal-gray trousers. He looked like someone halfway between a diplomat and a ghost. His posture was easy, but his eyes—those storm-blue eyes—stayed locked on her.

She painted for hours.

He watched her like she was working magic.

She studied him not like a lover, but like a language. Each brushstroke was a translation—his strength, his secrecy, the bruised parts he never spoke about. She painted the soft furrow in his brow that appeared when he was trying to read her. The slight curve of his mouth when he caught her watching him.

And then, in the background, she did something bold.

She painted a wall of color behind him—not a shadow, not steel, not gray. But blue. Not the blue of coldness.

The blue of sky.

The blue of freedom.

And in his chest, she added something almost invisible. A light, just beneath the surface. A glow.

He didn't notice it until she unveiled the finished canvas three days later.

---

When she pulled the cloth off the portrait, Nan didn't speak right away.

He stepped closer.

Looked hard.

Then softly asked, "Is that how you see me?"

Elara nodded.

"You don't paint men like they are," he said, voice low. "You paint them like you believe they could be."

She stepped toward him, brush still in hand. "That's the difference between a mirror and a portrait."

He turned to her, jaw tight with something he rarely let rise.

Emotion.

"You saw me," he whispered.

"From the beginning," she said. "Even when you tried to disappear."

---

He pulled her into him then—not out of passion, but reverence. He held her like someone who had been chosen. And she let him, painting her hands over his spine as if committing him to memory.

The portrait stayed in the studio, hung just across from her easel. Not for galleries. Not for clients.

Just for her.

A reminder that even those who live in silence can be seen clearly when the right eyes are looking.

CHAPTER TWENTY-FOUR

# The Interference
## (with full confession: "I was waiting for this moment my whole life")

Elara knew something was wrong the moment Nan canceled their dinner—for the third time in a week.

"Emergency. I'll explain later."

But he didn't. And when she called, it went to voicemail. Twice.

The silence wasn't new. She'd learned early that being with Nan meant accepting gaps. Delays. Things unsaid. But this time, it didn't feel like absence.

It felt like distance.

She didn't paint that night. Couldn't. Her brush hovered, paralyzed by worry she couldn't name. So she cleaned the studio instead. Then repainted a corner that didn't need repainting. Then opened her old sketchbooks, looking for something to ground her.

The next day, she received an envelope slid under her studio door.

No name. No return address. Just her name in block print.

Inside was a photograph.

Grainy. Surveillance-quality.

Nan. On a street corner. Talking to someone in a long coat. Another man she didn't recognize—military posture, dark sunglasses, a scar at his temple.

Written on the back, in the same hand:
"Do you really know who he works for?"

Her chest tightened.

She stared at the photo for a long time. Her first instinct was to call him. Demand answers.

But something stopped her.

She realized, for the first time since their story began, that she had no idea what Nan truly did.

She knew the titles. The vague phrases. "Intelligence," "field support," "international affairs." But the full truth?

He had never told her.

And she had never asked.

---

When he finally appeared at her studio late that night, he looked drained. Hollow behind the eyes. His jacket was soaked from the rain, and he didn't speak right away.

Elara stood in the doorway, arms crossed, the photograph clutched behind her back.

"I need to ask you something," she said.

Nan nodded, already bracing.

"Who do you really work for?"

His jaw clenched. Then he stepped inside, dripping.

"Elara, if I tell you, I put you at risk."

"You already did," she said, holding up the photograph. "Someone put this under my door. They know who you are. And now, they know who I am."

His face paled.

She watched him. Waiting.

And then, slowly, he spoke.

"I work for a division of international counter-threat intelligence. Covert. Off-book. Some of the people I report to don't technically exist. And yes—I've been watched. I'm still watched."

She didn't blink. "Was I part of your assignment?"

"No," he said instantly. "God, no. You were never a job. You were the one thing I ran from, and somehow… the one thing I always found my way back to."

She stood frozen.

He took a step closer. Then another.

"I've loved you," he said, voice beginning to tremble. "Since we were kids. Since summer school, when you used to paint galaxies in the margins of your notebooks. Since that night I kissed your neck and pretended I was brave."

She lowered her eyes—remembering.

"I tried to forget you," he said. "Tried to bury it. The work helped. Missions helped. But no matter where I went—Zurich, Cairo, Paris—if I closed my eyes, I saw you. I saw us."

She turned to him finally, her blue eyes full of storm.

"And now?" she whispered.

He reached for her hand, pressed it to his chest.

"Now I know," he said, barely breathing, "I was waiting for this moment my whole life."

She stood frozen in it. The rain on the windows. The paintbrush in her hand forgotten. The truth, laid bare.

"You're not safe," she said, voice cracking.

"I'm not trying to be," he said. "I'm trying to be yours. Wherever you go, I will find you. Just like I did now."

She searched his face.

And found no shadows there—only light that had waited too long to be seen.

NOT EVEN SILENCE STAYED EMPTY

"I'm not trying to be," he said. "I'm trying to be yours. Wherever you go, I will find you. Just like I did now."

She searched his face.

## CHAPTER TWENTY-FIVE

# The Threshold

It began with a sound.

Not loud. Not violent. Just... wrong.

Elara was locking up her studio late one night, lights already off, when she heard a click behind her. A pause. The faintest shifting of weight. She froze, hand on the doorknob, breath caught mid-movement.

She turned slowly.

No one was there.

But the air felt watched.

---

That same night, Nan received a call. An encrypted line he hadn't used in over a year.

> "They know, Malik. She's marked."

> "Who?"

> "Elara."

He didn't ask how. He didn't waste time arguing.

He ran.

---

He arrived at her place out of breath, heart in his throat. She opened the door before he knocked, like she'd been waiting.

"I think someone's been watching the studio," she said quietly.

"I know someone has."

He stepped in, checked every window, every lock, every corner of shadow. His hands were steady, but his eyes burned.

She followed him through the apartment, her voice calm—but inside, everything was cracking open.

"Nan," she said, after he'd secured the space. "I need to tell you something."

He turned.

Her hand went to her stomach but he didn't say that She was "pregnant." That night of Washington DC.

The world held its breath. Don't get too stressed he said. I'm here to protect you.

He stared at her, stunned. Then a thousand emotions flickered through his face—shock, fear, wonder, guilt, love.

"She didn't tell nothing to him. She wanted to be sure. And maybe... She wanted to see who he really was before She puts that kind of truth between them."

Tears welled in her eyes. Not fear. Weight.

"But I can't wait anymore, Nan. Because whoever's watching us isn't just watching me now."

He crossed the room in two steps, pulled her into him, holding her like she might vanish. His voice cracked against her hair.

"I was waiting my whole life for you," he said again.

Then he pulled back, eyes hardening.

"But we can't stay here."

She nodded. She already knew.

---

They left within the hour.

Nan had safehouses. Codes. Names that weren't names.

Elara packed only what mattered—her sketchbook, a folded photo of her parents, and one small pair of knitted booties she hadn't yet had the courage to show anyone.

The world they built in paint and song was behind them now.

The world ahead?

It would test them.

Hunt them.

But it would never break them.

Because now, they weren't running as two even if he didn't know it.

They were running as three or more even they both now don't know?

**Subject: Novel Chapter 26**

This chaptet raises the emotional and physical stakes dramatically, while also grounding Nan's silence and inner turmoil in real trauma. Chapter Twenty-Six: Kraków to reflect that Nan had just returned from three intense weeks in Ukraine, where a bombing injured him—a wound he's trying to hide even as he carries it with him.

## CHAPTER TWENTY-SIX

# Kraków, Poland
## (With Nan's Time in Ukraine and Injury)

Kraków in early spring was stone and silence, cold light slanting over old rooftops and tram wires. The city wore its history like a second skin—elegant, scarred, and unflinching.

Nan had just come from Ukraine.

He hadn't seen Elara in three weeks.

Three weeks of front-line whispers, midnight extractions, and air raid sirens that turned your blood to ice. There had been a mission gone wrong near Kramatorsk. A building targeted. A bomb—Russian-made—landed less than twenty meters from his team during a night recon.

The pressure had thrown him into a wall.

A shard of something—metal, glass, maybe concrete—cut deep above his right brow. He hadn't blacked out. But close. He wrapped it himself. Kept moving. When Gary his friend found him the next morning, he was blood-dried and still scanning rooftops like they were breathing.

The doctors in Kyiv stitched him in silence. No time for rest.

And now, not even time for healing.

The scar was fading, but still red and raw near his temple. His body ached with every step.

But his mind was fixed on only one thing:

Elara.

___________________________________________

They had arranged to meet in Kraków, safer ground. Elara would fly in from Vienna. Nan and Gary crossed from Lviv by train—quiet car, old steel, and guarded eyes.

Her flight was delayed.

Then again.

And again.

Nan checked the arrivals screen like a man trying to hold back a storm with logic. His shoulder throbbed. His head still rang some nights, especially in silence. But it wasn't pain that made him pace.

It was her absence.

"She's okay," Gary said, not looking up from his phone.

"You don't know that."

"I know you look like you haven't slept since Dnipro."

Nan didn't answer.

---

Elara arrived nearly three hours late.

Hair tousled. Coat wrinkled. Her blue eyes instantly scanning the terminal until they locked onto his.

She hurried to him—and stopped.

Her eyes caught the edge of the bandage still taped under his hair.

"What happened?" she whispered.

"Later," he said, pulling her close. "I just need to feel you right now."

---

They stayed at a small, elegant hotel off the Planty, a quiet circle of green space that wrapped the old town like an arm. The room had old oak floors and a balcony just wide enough for two.

That night, as she slept curled beside him in one of his shirts, Nan sat up in bed, staring out the window. The ache behind his temple pulsed softly.

He hadn't told her everything.

Not yet.

The bomb. The way Gary thought he'd died when they lost him in the dust. The way the world looked quieter after an explosion. Like something had been stripped away forever.

He didn't know how to speak that kind of weight.

Not yet.

But he would.

---

The next day, he found her missing suitcase himself—after three phone calls, one bribe, and a full trip back to the airport. When she saw it by the door that morning, her breath caught.

"You didn't have to do that."

"Yes," he said simply. "I did."

---

That afternoon, the three of them—Elara, Nan, and Gary—walked Kraków's quiet streets. Gary chatted casually, trying to keep the tone light, but Nan barely listened.

He was watching her.

The way her pace slowed.

The way she brushed her hand across her stomach when she thought he wasn't looking.

And suddenly—his chest tightened.

Not from pain.

But from knowing.

---

Later that evening, when Gary left for Lublin, Elara and Nan stood alone in the lobby, dusk filtering through the windows.

"You okay?" she asked softly, her hand brushing his as they stood shoulder to shoulder.

He looked down at her, at her blue eyes, at the faint curve of her body beneath her coat.

And he knew.

He didn't ask.

He didn't press.

He just kissed her forehead, gently, near the scar she hadn't yet seen in full.

And whispered into her hair:

"You don't have to say it. I already know."

## CHAPTER TWENTY-SEVEN

# The Decision
# (With Anny, Camille, and Elara's wish)

They sat in silence on the hotel balcony in Marseille, France two months later. A different country. A different phase of their lives.

The ocean stretched beyond the terracotta rooftops—blue and endless, calm in a way neither of them had been in weeks. The city moved slowly below: lavender carts in the market, bicycles rattling down narrow streets, music drifting from a café.

Elara's hand rested gently over her stomach now. The curve unmistakable. No more hiding. No more silence.

The baby—or so Nan believed—had started to move a few days earlier. He'd felt the flutter beneath her skin with wonder in his eyes, like he'd touched a miracle and didn't want to breathe too loud for fear of losing it.

But Elara had kept one last secret.

Just a little longer.

---

Now, at dusk, Nan sat beside her on the narrow balcony bench, a weathered file folder in his lap—worn, stamped, and trembling with old danger. Safehouse coordinates. Cut IDs. Escape plans that tasted more like exile.

"You still have the option to disappear," he said quietly.

"I know."

"They'd protect you. Even after Ukraine. You could go dark. Start over. South America. Iceland. I'd make it happen."

She didn't answer immediately. She watched him instead—his fingers still bruised from the field, the scar near his temple healing slow, his face caught between resolve and exhaustion.

She reached over, touched his hand.

"What about you?"

"I'd go," he said. "Anywhere. But I'd never stop looking over my shoulder."

"That's not what a child needs," she said softly.

"No," he agreed. "It's not."

---

The wind turned cooler. Light fell gold on her skin. And slowly, her expression shifted from caution to clarity.

"We can't be ghosts anymore," she said. "We can't raise a child in shadows. I want our baby to grow up with walls they can paint on. With birthdays. With roots. Not passwords."

Nan looked at her.

Deeply.

And for the first time in years, she saw his fear fade into something else:

Hope.

"And if danger comes back?" he asked.

She reached again, placing his palm against her belly.

Only this time—he felt it.

Two movements.

Not one.

His brow furrowed. Eyes lifting slowly. Searching her face.

"Elara..."

She smiled—gentle, proud, full of light.

"I was waiting for the right moment," she whispered. "We're having twins."

His breath caught.

"What?"

Her smile widened, eyes shimmering. "Two heartbeats. I've known since Kraków. I just... needed to be sure you were really here before I gave you all of it."

He covered his face with one hand, overwhelmed, then leaned forward and pressed his forehead to her belly—laughing, crying, and whispering something only they would remember.

"You've always given me more than I ever thought I deserved," he said.

"No," she whispered back. "I'm giving you exactly what you're ready for."

---

That night, they made the call.

Nan contacted an old handler—someone he trusted with his life—and said the words he never thought he'd say.

"I'm done."

And Elara opened her sketchbook. On the first page, written in charcoal, were the names she hadn't yet shown him:

Anny – "grace."

His daughter. The one he'd dreamed of for years without daring to hope.

And beneath it:

Camille – "the one who is free."
Her son. Gentle strength. A quiet fire wrapped in softness.

Twins.

Two names.

Two lives.

His daughter. Her son.

Born of storm.

Bound for light.

And as Nan read the names, still speechless, Elara leaned into his shoulder, a quiet smile dancing at the edge of her lips.

"We're not done, you know," she murmured.

He turned. "What do you mean?"

She looked at him sideways, blue eyes twinkling with mischief and certainty.

"We need a third," she said. "Alexander-Aris. We have to be five. It's my lucky number."

He stared at her, stunned. Then grinned. A slow, reckless, beautiful grin.

"You want three?"

"I want everything," she said.

And as the sun dropped beyond the edge of the sea, he kissed her deeply—knowing that she wasn't just building a home.

She was building a future.

And he was finally part of it.

## CHAPTER TWENTY-EIGHT

# Blood and Light

It began in the early hours of a gray morning in Marseille.

Elara's breath caught mid-sentence at the kitchen table. A hand went to her belly. Her eyes widened—not with panic, but with that primal, ancient knowing only mothers carry. Pain clenched around her ribs like a vise. The table shook. The teacup shattered.

Nan dropped his phone before it hit the floor.

The drive to the hospital blurred into red lights and white knuckles. No music. Just Elara's sharp breaths, counted out like seconds on a bomb.

She had gone into labor three weeks early.

---

Anny came first.

But not gently.

She was turned wrong—high and stubborn. The labor was long. Brutal. Hours stretched into eternity. Elara's screams cracked glass. Her body buckled. Blood pressure dropped. Her eyes flickered between worlds.

The doctors moved fast.

A decision.

Emergency cesarean.

Nan was pushed behind the curtain, gloved hands trembling. They worked quickly, precisely—but Anny was tangled. The umbilical cord coiled tight. There was blood. Too much.

Then, finally—a cry. Loud. Piercing. Alive.

Anny.

Then a second.

Camille. Smaller. Slippery. Breathing.

But Elara...

Elara was bleeding too fast.

A rupture. A drop. A whisper.

She drifted.

---

In the darkness between anesthesia and waking, her mind went back. Far back.

To her birth country.

To alleys where she ran barefoot under curfews.
To men who chased her for what she believed, not what she'd done.
To interrogations disguised as conversations.
To artists disappeared.
To nights when she had packed her life into a backpack and prayed she'd still be alive by dawn.

Pain in her womb mirrored the trauma in her history.

And there—lying between life and death—she made a wish.

And a curse.

To her daughter, Anny.

"You will not return there. You will not be chased. You will not carry the ghosts I bled to leave behind."

She had chosen to give birth in a foreign land on purpose.

Not for beauty.

For safety.

Her children would never be born under the flags that once hunted their mother.

---

She woke on the third day.

Weak.

Tethered to tubes.

Alive.

Nan sat beside her, their children asleep in his arms—two bundles of breath and beginning.

Her voice was cracked when she whispered, "I'm still here."

He leaned forward, eyes full of salt and awe. "You fought harder than anyone I've ever known."

She didn't cry.

But she looked at Anny—tiny and fierce, asleep in pink—and whispered, "You'll never know the streets that tried to silence me."

A vow. A protection.

A shield of distance made from blood and love.

---

Elara stayed in the hospital eight days. Her legs didn't hold her weight for twenty-one. The pain was sharp, but memory was sharper.

She carried them both now—her children, and her past.

But she would only pass down one.

---

When she finally stood again, Nan was holding Camille. Anny lay sleeping in a bassinet, fists curled like a fighter.

And Elara said, through tears, through steel:

"See? Told you five was my number."

**Subject: Novel Chapter 29 -" The Telling"**

This is a deeply touching addition. The presence of Elara's late father—even in absence—adds quiet gravity to her motherhood and legacy. Her writing a biography for her children is a beautiful act of remembrance and love, ensuring that memory lives where voice cannot. Here's an enriched version of Chapter Twenty-Nine, now with her father's passing and the book she wrote for her children.

## CHAPTER TWENTY-NINE

# The Telling
## (With Alexander, Aris, Antoni and Chris, and the memory of her father)

The farmhouse they lived in now sat on a hill just outside of Avignon.

It wasn't large. It wasn't grand. But it had sun in the windows, dirt on the floor, and walls filled with the kind of quiet you could grow a childhood in.

Anny was five.

Camille, by a few soft minutes, was still technically "the little one," though he never let anyone forget he'd been the first to speak.

They had Nan's sharp perception and Elara's fierce will. Their blue eyes sparkled with mischief. Their laughter ran through the house like birdsong.

And on one particular rainy afternoon, Anny crawled onto her mother's lap with a question Elara hadn't expected to hear yet.

"Maman," she asked, curling into her, "where were you born?"

Elara paused.

They were sitting by the window, the storm drumming gently on the glass. Camille was asleep nearby, curled into a blanket with his toy lion. Nan was in the next room, humming as he sorted books that didn't need sorting.

Elara looked down at her daughter.

And for a long moment, said nothing.

Anny tilted her head. "Did it rain there too?"

Elara smiled softly. "Sometimes. But the thunder there was louder. And it didn't always come from the sky."

Anny blinked, wide-eyed. "Was it scary?"

Elara wrapped her arms around her.

"It was a place with beauty... and shadows. I loved it once. But I had to leave so I could become your maman."

Anny thought about that, five years old but already built for wonder.

"Is that why we live here?"

Elara nodded. "We live here because I want you to paint the sky without fear. Because your name was spoken before you ever cried. Because this is a place where you are free."

She didn't say exile. Didn't say censorship. Didn't mention the fences she jumped to become a mother in the sun.

Not yet.

But one day she would.

---

Later that evening, the wind had quieted, and Nan stood with her on the porch. His hands wrapped around her waist, resting over the gentle rise of her belly.

"Alexander and Aris are getting closer," she whispered, smiling.

He smiled. "I still can't believe it. Another pair of twins."

Elara leaned into him, but her smile faded to something softer.

"I wish my father could meet them," she said.

Nan said nothing for a moment. Just held her.

"He would've loved them," she went on. "He would've sat in that garden and told Camille stories until he fell asleep. Anny would've followed him around like a shadow."

Her voice trembled. "He died the year after they were born. Quietly. He never got to hold them."

Nan kissed her temple. "They'll still know him."

"They will," she said. "Because I wrote him down."

She slipped from his arms, stepped inside briefly, and returned with a thick, cloth-bound book. The title was hand-lettered in soft black ink: "The Hands That Planted Me: Stories of My Father."

"I wrote it for them," she whispered. "So even if they never hear his voice, they'll know who he was. How he rebuilt our fence. How he held me when I couldn't walk. How he told me, when I was fifteen and angry and ready to run, 'You are not alone, mija.'"

Nan took the book. Opened it. Inside were sketches, pages of memory, pieces of Elara only her father had seen.

"They'll know him," she said, "because I carry him."

---

She rested a hand on her belly.

"Alexander and Aris will know all of them. Even Antoni and Chris(her nephews). Even the life I ran from."

"You think they'll understand?" Nan asked.

"They'll feel it in the quiet between pages," she said. "And maybe, someday, they'll go find the pieces I left behind."

---

Inside her, two more heartbeats pulsed in time with the past.

And in the room behind her, her children slept safe in a life their grandfather never got to see—but helped build with every sacrifice.

---

We add a vivid, emotional story from Elara's past—something she includes in the biography of her father, or recalls while sitting in quiet reflection. This memory will connect her past and present, showing her courage, the weight she carried, and why she protects her children with such fierce tenderness.

Here is the continuation of Chapter Twenty-Nine, with Elara's story from the past woven in:

---

Elara stood alone in the children's room after they had gone to sleep—books still open, socks on the floor, Anny's curls tangled in her pillow, Camille's arms wrapped around a stuffed elephant.

She pressed her hand against the windowpane, watching the moon rise over the vineyard.

Her other hand rested on her belly.

Alexander and Aris.

She knew their names. She could feel their rhythm. But tonight, her thoughts slipped backward—toward a time when she had no names to protect, only fire to survive.

A single page of her father's biography remained tucked in her sketchbook. One she hadn't included in the printed edition.

A story about her.

---

Elara, age 23:

The border crossing had been unmarked, a dirt path along a pine-choked ridge. She had one backpack. One name. One secret she refused to give up.

A friend—gone now—had slipped her forged papers in a café, folded into a napkin. "Don't say your name," he warned. "Don't look anyone in the eye unless you want them to remember you."

She remembered the frost that bit through her coat as she waited in line, the cold bite of suspicion in the soldier's stare. He was young. Too young to be so cold. But his fingers rested on the trigger of his rifle like it was an extension of his fear.

He asked her three questions.

She lied twice.

But on the third—he asked, "Why are you leaving?"

She froze.

Then answered softly, "Because my voice is louder than they like."

The boy stared at her for a long time. Too long.

Then, without a word, he stamped her papers.

And let her go.

She walked across the border with her throat burning and a new name clutched in her fist.

---

Back in the quiet farmhouse, she sat on the floor beside Camille's bed and opened her sketchbook.

She copied that page by hand.

And wrote beneath it, in her softest ink:

> "To my children: If you ever wonder why I stayed quiet for so long— it's because the loudest things I've ever said were not with my mouth, but with my feet. I walked away to build you something better."

She closed the sketchbook.

Kissed both sleeping children.

And whispered, "You are free because I ran."

---

Let's craft another defining scene from Elara's past—a moment that shaped her voice, her rage, and her quiet decision to resist. This one takes place before she fled, when she was still a rising artist in her home country—still visible, still vulnerable.

This memory could be one she writes in a hidden chapter of her father's biography or quietly recounts to Nan years later—when the children are asleep and the house is full, but the past still hums like an old scar.

Memory: The Mural That Disappeared

Elara was nineteen when she painted her first public mural.

It was allowed—technically. Commissioned by the local arts council as part of a "youth beautification" initiative. A wall no one cared about, in a neighborhood most of the country pretended didn't exist.

She didn't paint flowers.

She didn't paint flags.

She painted a woman with no mouth and hands raised to the sky— hands turning into birds. Around her, children floated in shades of gold and blue, each with paint dripping from their fingertips like they had just rewritten the world.

It wasn't political.

But it was powerful.

Too powerful.

Within two days, a minister called it "inappropriate."

By the end of the week, police had come by her university studio.

They didn't arrest her. That would've been too obvious.

Instead, they took her brushes.

They "accidentally" erased her scholarship records.

And the mural?

Painted over in gray before the month was done.

———————————————————————————————————————

She cried the night they destroyed it. Not loud. Not in protest. Just… silently. In her father's kitchen. Her hands still stained with cobalt and ochre.

Her father poured her tea. Said nothing.

But before he left the room, he put something in her hand.

A small canvas.

One he'd quietly peeled from the wall before the erasers came.

A piece of the sky she painted.

Intact.

"You may lose walls," he told her. "But never your color."

———————————————————————————————————————

Years later, in her farmhouse in France, Elara kept that scrap of sky tucked behind glass above her writing desk.

Anny once asked, "What's that blue for?"

Elara just smiled.

"For everything they tried to take."

---

We continue with another defining moment from Elara's past—this time, a moment of voice, not just art. A time when she stood in front of a crowd and spoke, not with paint, but with words—risking everything for truth. This story would live in memory, or perhaps be part of the secret final chapter of her father's biography, saved for the children when they are old enough to understand what courage sounds like.

---

Memory: The Night of the Poem

Elara was twenty-one when she read a poem in public for the first—and only—time in her home country.

It was at an open mic in a tucked-away café, hosted by a forgotten artist collective in the basement of an old bookstore. Dust coated the wine bottles, and the lights were too dim to feel safe. But the room pulsed with quiet fire. Everyone there knew what was at stake.

She hadn't planned to speak.

She had come to listen.

To disappear.

But when someone called her name—her real one, her full one—she couldn't refuse. She stood. Walked to the microphone with knees like paper. Opened her notebook with hands that barely stopped shaking.

And read a piece she wrote the night a journalist vanished from the radio.

She didn't name names.

Didn't shout.

She simply told a story about a bird who stopped singing because the wind told it to, and how silence spread through the forest like frost, until one morning, a child woke up and could no longer remember music.

When she finished, the room was dead silent.

Then someone clapped.

Then another.

And another.

It lasted only a minute—but that minute cost her everything.

___________________________________________

Two nights later, two men followed her home.

They didn't touch her.

They didn't speak.

They just let her see them.

A warning.

A promise.

That night, she packed everything she owned into a single suitcase. Burned the poem. And left.

———

She never read aloud in public again.

Not even after she crossed the border.

But years later, in a farmhouse in Avignon, her daughter Anny would find a recording of that night tucked inside a notebook. A scratchy, half-lost file.

"Maman," she would ask. "Is that your voice?"

Elara would nod.

"That was the first time I was truly afraid."

"But you didn't stop," Anny would say.

"No," Elara would answer. "I just changed how I sang."

———

Let's complete this final memory with a tender, direct message from Elara to her children, drawn from the depth of everything she's survived—and everything she's chosen for them. It's not just a closing—it's a legacy of love, spoken from a woman who walked through fire and chose gentleness anyway.

Here is the version of the story "The Shoes on the Fence", now ending with her words of unconditional, unforgettable love:

Memory: The Shoes on the Fence

Elara was sixteen.

It was the year her mother had started working nights. Her father was recovering from an injury—one that left him quiet and slow-moving, his strong hands trembling sometimes when he reached for his tea.

Money was thin.

Some nights, so was food.

And Elara had one pair of shoes.

They were canvas, soft-soled, and worn so thin her toes peeked through when she walked. She never complained. Never asked for another pair. She just painted them. Every weekend. New colors, new symbols, new stories in brushstrokes.

"A silent rebellion".

One afternoon, on her way home from school, she passed the house with the ivy-covered fence—the one with the lemon tree, the sleeping dog, and the old woman who never spoke to anyone.

On the fence that day hung a pair of shoes.

Leather. Hand-stitched. Her exact size.

With a note tucked into one:

> "Paint these too. But only when you're ready to walk somewhere new."

She never found out who left them.

But she wore them for years.

She painted the soles with stars.

---

The night she fled her country at twenty-three, she placed the shoes in a bag.

They were the only thing she kept from her old life.

Years later, Nan found them in a box in the attic of the farmhouse.

"These yours?" he asked, holding them up.

Elara nodded slowly. "They helped me run."

He looked closer—saw the faded stars along the soles, barely there but still visible.

"You didn't paint over them."

"No," she said. "They reminded me that someone once believed I'd get out."

---

That night, as rain tapped the windows and the twins slept soundly in the next room, she sat by the fire, shoes in her lap, whispering stories to herself.

Not of the running.

But of the small grace that carried her when she thought no one saw her feet bleeding.

---

Now she tells her children:

> "Sometimes the loudest hope is the kind that leaves you shoes and never says a word.
Sometimes love doesn't shout—it waits. It protects. It lets you go until you're ready to return."

And then she says to them—

> "I would burn through the world to keep you safe.
I would break my body in half to carry you through the dark.
You are the reason I left.
You are the reason I stayed gone.
And you are the reason I became everything I never thought I could be."

> "I love you more than memory.
More than blood.
More than the stories they will tell about me when I am gone."

# CHAPTER THIRTY

# Arrival

The morning Elara gave birth to Alexander and Aris, the house was quiet.

Too quiet.

The world outside the farmhouse lay wrapped in a thin mist. The trees were still. The children's drawings hung on the fridge. A kettle hissed in the kitchen—forgotten.

Nan found her leaning against the wall in the hallway, hands on her belly, face pale but composed.

"It's time," she said softly.

He didn't panic.

He didn't run.

He simply wrapped her coat around her shoulders, kissed her forehead, and whispered, "We've done this before. But this time, we're ready."

---

At the hospital in Avignon, the nurses greeted her like a returning friend. She'd been monitored for weeks—no risks taken this time. No room for fear to grow wild.

But as the contractions came stronger, and the pain rose like a tide, Elara slipped into silence.

She wasn't afraid.

She was remembering.

The scar from her last birth pulled tight across her abdomen. The old ache. The memories. But she focused on the now—on Nan's voice. On her breathing. On the lives inside her, pushing toward light.

---

Alexander came first.

He was broad-shouldered, deep-eyed, and howled the moment air touched his lungs.

Elara sobbed when she saw him. "He looks like my father," she whispered, and Nan smiled through tears.

Moments later came Aris.

Quieter.

Lighter.

Born with a soft cry and wide, alert eyes—as if he already knew everything and was just waiting to arrive.

Elara held both of them in her arms before she let herself sleep.

Nan kissed her hand and pressed his forehead to hers.

"You gave us the whole sky," he whispered.

---

Three days later, when they brought the babies home, Anny and Camille stood in the doorway with handmade crowns and signs that said Welcome Our Brothers!

Camille immediately claimed Aris as "his twin." Anny refused to stop staring at Alexander.

Nan looked around the room—four children now, laughter spilling from corners, artwork pinned to every wall, Elara radiant and tired and stronger than ever—and thought:

This is what survival becomes when love takes over.

---

Let's deepen the emotional truth of that final moment—not just a shift in the kind of fight Elara now faces, but a soul-deep realization of what it means to protect not just lives, but spirits, stories, and the possibility of peace.

Here is the final enriched ending to Chapter Thirty: Arrival, now pulsing with emotional weight and quiet fire:

---

That night, when the house went still, Elara stood by the window holding both babies. Outside, the stars blinked like they remembered her story.

She whispered into the warm space between her sons' faces:

> "You were born into a world I built from rubble.
You were born not to flee, but to grow.
You were born for light.
And I will never stop loving you—not even when the world forgets my name."

And with both twins resting on her chest, Elara finally closed her eyes.

Not to escape.

But to rest.

Because the story no longer needed to be fought for—
or perhaps, because a new fight had quietly begun.

Not with fists or flights.

But with hands that soothe.

With voices that teach.

With the terrifying, beautiful responsibility of shaping souls instead of surviving systems.

A fight to raise children who will not carry the fear she once slept beside.
A fight to teach truth in a world that so easily forgets.
A fight to stay soft in a world that wants her hard.
A fight to love—boldly, daily, loudly—when the world still sometimes punishes love that doesn't fit inside flags.

She would rise again and again.

For scraped knees. For broken crayons. For loud questions. For quiet heartbreaks.

She would rise.

Because this fight was not the end of her story.

It was her legacy.

To raise all her children not in the shadow of what she escaped,
but in the full sunlight of everything she became.

And for that—

she was ready.

# EPILOGUE

# The Sky She Painted
## (from Anny)

I was sixteen when I read the last page of her book.

Not the one she published.

The one she kept hidden, deep in the back of her drawer. The one none of us were supposed to find. Torn corners, pages full of her handwriting—the kind she only used when she thought no one was watching. There were places where the ink bled from tears. Places where she'd started a sentence and couldn't finish it.

Camille found the "key".

Of course he did.

We sat on the floor of her study, our backs against the bookcase. The twins were outside, chasing each other through the olive trees. Papa was asleep in his chair, his hand still curled like it used to when he held her fingers.

The light was soft. Dust danced in it.

And I turned the page.

And read.

And everything I thought I understood about my mother... came undone.

---

She had written everything.

About the mural they erased.
About the night she read a poem that got her followed.
About the time she ran barefoot down a border road with her name hidden in her sock.
About how she bled for me—almost died for me—before she ever heard me cry.

And about how terrified she was that we'd never know her.
Not really.

Not the parts she didn't show in the daylight.

Not the parts she buried beneath warm breakfasts and bedtime songs.

---

At the bottom of the last page, she had written this:

> "To Anny. To Camille. To Alexander and Aris.
You are my sky. You are the proof that I was here.
I hope one day you forgive the silences I kept.
I hope you feel the love I buried in every one."

---

I pressed my face to the page.

And cried like I was five again.

Because I remembered every morning she brushed my hair,
every moment she reached for me when I didn't know I needed her,
every time she said "I'm here" without needing to say anything else.

And I realized:

She had never hidden anything.

She had just carried it so I wouldn't have to.

---

People ask me what kind of mother she was.

And I tell them—

She was the kind who made safety feel sacred.
The kind who let love be fierce.
The kind who taught us that silence can be holy,
and survival can be art.

She didn't just raise us.

She shielded us with her own life.

She didn't just tell us to be strong.

She showed us what it looked like to be soft and still survive.

---

Camille paints now. So do I.

Sometimes we work side by side in her old studio.

The brushes feel like hers.
The colors still carry her breath.
And sometimes, when the light hits the canvas just right, I swear—
it's her hand guiding mine.

Papa says I have her eyes.
But I think what I really carry is her courage.

She gave it to all of us.

And she gave it without asking anything back.

---

The sky she painted?

It's still above us.

And we are still walking in her light.

---

## CHAPTER THIRTY-ONE

# The Quiet Inheritance
## (from Camille)

It's late.

The kind of late where everything softens. The kitchen hums. The olive trees don't move. Even the twins are finally still, their wild feet tucked under tangled blankets in the next room.

And Mama is painting.

Again.

I should be asleep. But I've been watching her from the hallway for an hour. She doesn't know. Or maybe she does and pretends not to. That's her way. She lets me keep my silences like others keep secrets.

The canvas is tall and pale. She hasn't touched it in days. Tonight, she moves slowly. Not with hesitation—but care. Every brushstroke lands like memory. She doesn't blink much when she paints. She looks like she's praying.

I think, sometimes, that she is.

---

People say I'm like her. I don't always see it. I'm quieter. I don't like questions. I don't like noise.

But I carry something I don't have a name for.
A kind of weight.
A kind of wind at my back I didn't choose.
It doesn't hurt.
But it never leaves.

I think it's Her "FIRE".

But cooled, like stone.

---

She used to tuck me in when I was little and say, "The world doesn't always love the soft ones. So we love each other twice as hard."

I never forgot that.

---

Tonight, I walk into the studio without asking.

She doesn't turn.

She knows it's me.

"Couldn't sleep?" she asks, still painting.

"No."

She pauses. Dips her brush in a color I can't name.

"I thought you'd come."

I sit on the stool by the window.

"Why do you paint at night?" I ask.

She smiles—just a little. Still focused.

"Because the world doesn't interrupt me."

I nod. That makes sense.

---

She finally sets the brush down. Steps back. It's not finished. But it's something.

It's a woman, half-formed in gold and shadow, standing in the middle of a burning field.

But she's not running.

She's singing.

Mama looks at me then.

And I see it in her eyes.

The tiredness. The joy. The miles.

The love.

All of it.

She steps over to me. Brushes my hair back like she used to. Kisses my forehead.

"You feel too much," she says gently.

"So do you," I whisper.

She smiles.

"Maybe that's our strength."

## CHAPTER THIRTY-ONE

# The Quiet Inheritance
## (from Camille)

It's late.

The kind of late where everything softens. The kitchen hums. The olive trees don't move. Even the twins are finally still, their wild feet tucked under tangled blankets in the next room.

And Mama is painting.

Again.

I should be asleep. But I've been watching her from the hallway for an hour. She doesn't know. Or maybe she does and pretends not to. That's her way. She lets me keep my silences like others keep secrets.

The canvas is tall and pale. She hasn't touched it in days. Tonight, she moves slowly. Not with hesitation—but care. Every brushstroke lands like memory. She doesn't blink much when she paints. She looks like she's praying.

I think, sometimes, that she is.

---

People say I'm like her. I don't always see it. I'm quieter. I don't like questions. I don't like noise.

But I carry something I don't have a name for.
A kind of weight.
A kind of wind at my back I didn't choose.
It doesn't hurt.
But it never leaves.

I think it's Her "FIRE".

But cooled, like stone.

---

She used to tuck me in when I was little and say, "The world doesn't always love the soft ones. So we love each other twice as hard."

I never forgot that.

---

Tonight, I walk into the studio without asking.

She doesn't turn.

She knows it's me.

"Couldn't sleep?" she asks, still painting.

"No."

She pauses. Dips her brush in a color I can't name.

"I thought you'd come."

I sit on the stool by the window.

"Why do you paint at night?" I ask.

She smiles—just a little. Still focused.

"Because the world doesn't interrupt me."

I nod. That makes sense.

---

She finally sets the brush down. Steps back. It's not finished. But it's something.

It's a woman, half-formed in gold and shadow, standing in the middle of a burning field.

But she's not running.

She's singing.

Mama looks at me then.

And I see it in her eyes.

The tiredness. The joy. The miles.

The love.

All of it.

She steps over to me. Brushes my hair back like she used to. Kisses my forehead.

"You feel too much," she says gently.

"So do you," I whisper.

She smiles.

"Maybe that's our strength."

**Subject: Novel Chapter 33 - The Language of Her Silence (from Aris)**

Let's follow Aris a little longer—quietly, gently—as he begins to learn her language. He won't tell anyone at first. This chapter will be full of stillness, quiet determination, and a son's longing to understand the world his mother left behind... not through her voice, but through her words.

## CHAPTER THIRTY-THREE

# The Language of Her Silence
## (from Aris)

I didn't tell her.

Not the next day. Not the week after.

But I found a book in the back of Papa's study—old, cracked, filled with translations.

Her language.

The language she left behind.

It didn't look like much. Just pages of unfamiliar shapes, worn verbs, thick roots. But it felt like holding something forbidden and sacred.

Something I wasn't supposed to understand—but needed to.

---

I started slow.

One word at a time.
I whispered them to myself at night, under the covers.
I wrote them in chalk on the wall behind my bed, where no one would see.
I matched them to the old notebook from the box.
Matched meanings to emotion.
Shapes to tone.
I didn't need full grammar.

I just needed her voice.

Even if she never spoke it again.

---

One night I caught her standing in the hallway, staring at a painting. Her arms were crossed. Her eyes were soft. She looked like she was listening to something far away.

I didn't speak.

I just stood beside her.

And after a moment, I whispered:

> "To agapi sou den efige pote."

She turned slowly.

And I saw it.

The shock.
The recognition.
And then the tears.

She didn't ask how I knew. She didn't speak at all.

She just pulled me into her arms and held me there—

not like I was her little boy,

but like I was someone who had finally come home to her past.

---

That night, I dreamed in her language.

And it didn't sound foreign anymore.

It sounded like her laughter.

Like her lullabies.

Like the truth she had never spoken—

but always carried.

**Subject: Novel Chapter 34 The Story I Never Told (from Elara)**

Let's take this moment of quiet awakening and let it bloom into a family truth—a chapter where Elara gathers all her children, now old enough, and finally tells them the full story. Not as a warning. Not as a confession. But as a gift.

This will be a soft, emotional chapter—filled with fire, history, and love. The moment the silence finally breaks. We will add her relationship with her father, That adds even more depth to Elara's bond with her father—and why his quiet strength, his absence, and his eventual support meant so much to her. Let's fold that memory gently into Chapter Thirty-Four, giving it the emotional weight it deserves within her telling.

## KEY PART CHAPTER THIRTY-FOUR

# The Story I Never Told
## (from Elara) now including the truth about her father:

She asked them to meet her in the garden.

No one knew why.

Alexander brought his guitar. Aris had a notebook tucked under his arm. Camille came with paint still drying on his sleeve, and Anny—always aware, always listening—carried nothing but her breath.

The sun was low. The lavender was still. And Elara sat on the edge of the old stone bench with a folded piece of paper in her hand.

They hadn't seen her like this before.

Still. Heavy. Certain.

"Sit," she said.

They did.

No one spoke.

---

"For a long time," she began, "I thought the best way to protect you was to stay quiet."

Her voice didn't shake.

"But silence has weight too. It becomes a wall. A mirror. A second skin. And I've decided... I don't want you to grow up only knowing the version of me I created here."

Her fingers opened the folded paper.

There was writing on it—her old name, written in strong, slanted ink.

"This is who I was."

---

"This moment adds powerful emotional symmetry—just as Elara nearly lost her life giving birth to Anny, her own life began with the near-loss of her father. It weaves the theme of survival, sacrifice, and love across generations. Here's the memory inside Chapter Thirty-Four: The Story I Never Told, now including the moment Elara nearly lost her father when she was born":

---

She told them everything.

The mural.
The poem.
The shoes on the fence.
The boy with the gun at the border who let her through.
The fire. The fear. The way she crossed into another life without knowing if she'd ever be able to build one.

And then—her voice softened.

She looked down at the folded page in her hand, then up at her children. Her eyes shimmered like dusk over water.

She told them about her father.

> "He was a Captain in the navy.
Always gone. Always somewhere just beyond the horizon."

Her voice cracked—not from grief, but from longing.

> "When I was a child, I used to sit by the window for hours,
pretending the clouds were carrying him home.
I missed him so much, sometimes it felt like I couldn't breathe."

She paused, then added something none of them had ever heard before.

> "The day I was born… we almost lost him.
Someone tried to harm him.
A man from the neighborhood—someone angry after an argument
between families—stabbed him from behind.
Right outside our house."

> "He survived. But barely.
While my mother brought me into the world,
they were stitching him back into it across the city."

Her voice grew quiet.

> "So I was born between breath and blood.
Between entrance and exit.
And somehow… I think that's why I learned to hold life like it's fragile.
Because from my first moment, it almost slipped away."

**Subject: Novel Chapter 34 and a half - The Man Who Stayed ( by Nan )**

let's deepen Nan's chapter with more emotion and the tension between his past life and Elara's. Their love was powerful, but not without sharp edges. He was trained to erase; she was born to speak. And yet, they chose each other. This version of Chapter Thirty-Four and a Half: The Man Who Stayed gives Nan's voice more weight, contradiction, and quiet love.

## CHAPTER THIRTY-FOUR AND A HALF

# The Man Who Stayed
## (from Nan)

They don't ask me about my past.

Not often.

I think they know I'm still holding pieces of it close. Not out of shame—but out of habit.

Because for a long time, I wasn't built for this life.
I was trained for silence.
For calculation.
For leaving before anyone noticed I'd arrived.

I was a man of secrets.

And then I fell in love with a woman who bled truth.

---

Elara and I were never meant to work.

Her entire life was fire and color and voice.
Mine was shadows and locked doors and never being too visible for too long.

She used to say, "You disappear when you feel too much."
And I did.

Because I was taught that emotion was weakness.

That vulnerability could kill you.

But she made me feel too much.

So I started writing her letters.

---

We weren't always together—there were times I had to vanish, missions I couldn't explain, months when I had no way to see her. But I always found a way to write.

Sometimes from safehouses.
Sometimes from rooftops.
Once from the back of a truck leaving the eastern border.

And she always wrote back.

---

She never asked where I was.

She only ever wrote things like:

> "I'm painting you into my mornings."
"I'm still wearing the scarf you left behind."
"I don't need to know where you are—I just need to know you're still
walking toward me."

---

Her handwriting saved me more times than I can count.

It reminded me who I was becoming.

Not the ghost they trained me to be—
but the man she believed in.

Even when I didn't believe in myself.

---

We fought sometimes. Quietly, but hard.

She wanted to speak.
I wanted to protect her by keeping everything unspoken.

Her poems were dangerous.

My silences were worse.

She once told me, "You don't get to choose safety for me, Nan. I've
already chosen love over safety a thousand times."

And it broke me.

Because she was right.

---

I didn't know how to be open.

So I learned.

With her.

One quiet hour at a time.

One scar kissed.

One truth confessed.

One letter at a time.

---

When Anny was born, I saw her nearly slip away.
And I knew, in that sterile white room, what it meant to love someone without armor.

I held our daughter in my arms, but I couldn't take my eyes off Elara's face—
pale, still, trembling.

I begged the universe—just let her stay.

She did.

But something in me didn't.

The man I was before didn't survive that day.

---

Now I live in a house full of light.
Brushstrokes on the walls.
Laughter down the halls.
Words spoken without fear.

And sometimes I still wake up thinking I'm undercover.
But then I see her sleeping, hair across the pillow.
I hear Anny humming downstairs.
Camille mixing paint.
Aris flipping pages of his notebook.
Alexander tapping a rhythm on the table.

And I remember—

I'm not running anymore.

---

Our lives were once in conflict.
Her voice.
My silence.

But somehow—

Love made a bridge of those contradictions.

Now our children walk across it every day.

## CHAPTER THIRTY-FIVE

# What I Kept Quiet
## (from Anny)

The gallery was small.

Tucked between a bakery and a bookstore, with white walls and crooked light. The owner didn't ask many questions. She liked my sketches. Said they were "honest." I didn't know what that meant at first.

I do now.

---

My first show was called "Inheritance."

Camille helped me hang the pieces. Aris and Alexander carried the frames. Papa fixed the lighting. Mama stayed home until the day of the opening—she said she wanted the surprise to land.

But I think she just needed to be alone with her heartbeat for a while.

I understood that.

---

I didn't sign my full name on any of the paintings.

Just A. Fan.

I wanted them to find her in my work, not me.

Because she was the beginning.

Not just of our family—

But of everything I believe about survival, truth, and color.

---

The first piece they hung in the front window was titled The Woman and the Burning Field.

It was based on one of Mama's old unfinished canvases.

But this time, I painted her standing in the middle of the fire—

Not running.

Not afraid.

Singing.

---

The second was The Border Fence, with a pair of painted shoes hanging from the wire like prayer flags. Camille cried when I hung it.

The third?

The Four Who Watched Her Rise.

It was us. Me. Camille. Aris. Alexander.

All painted in soft gold, standing behind her like shadows made of light.

---

When Mama walked in that night and saw them—

She didn't speak.

She just stood in the center of the gallery and turned in slow circles, taking it all in.

And when she reached me, she touched my cheek, and whispered:

> "You didn't just tell my story.
You honored it."

I said:

> "No, Maman. I continued it."

## CHAPTER THIRTY-SIX

# The Room Where She Spoke for Me
## (from Nan)

I went before the opening.

Alone.

Anny didn't know.

Neither did Elara.

I told the gallery owner I was there to "check the lighting," and she nodded politely—too polite to ask questions. I've learned how to blend in, even now. Some habits die harder than others.

But the moment I walked in and saw that first canvas—

I forgot how to breathe.

---

It was the piece titled The Woman and the Burning Field.

But it wasn't just Elara.

It was all of us.

Her arms were lifted. Her feet bare. Her mouth open—singing or shouting, I couldn't tell.

But behind her—barely visible in layers of dark blue and ash-gray—was the outline of a man.

A man with no face.

Just hands, outstretched.

Trying to reach her through smoke.

I knew who he was.

She hadn't painted me clearly.

But I was there.

---

The second canvas was worse.

The Letters.

Dozens of scraps—painted to look like old paper—scattered across a wide canvas. Phrases layered in different handwritings. Some hers. Some mine.

> "I'm painting you into my mornings."
"Don't come back unless it's to stay."
"I never asked to feel this much."
"I never wanted anything else."

She had found them.

The letters.

All of them.

---

There was one painting—small, almost hidden near the corner—titled simply Father.

It was just a chair.

Worn leather. Shadowed. Empty.

But the light was falling on it like someone had just stood up.

Like someone was coming back.

And I stood in front of that painting longer than anything else.

Because somehow—

she had spoken for me.

In ways I never dared to speak for myself.

---

When I finally left the gallery, the sky had started to pink.

And I didn't say anything that night.

Not even to her.

I just kissed the top of her head at dinner, and she leaned into me for a second longer than usual.

That was enough.

## CHAPTER THIRTY-SEVEN

# The Wall No One Asked For
## (from Camille)

There's a wall behind Mama's studio.

Old stone. Cracked in places. Covered in ivy.

No one uses it. No one talks about it. It's just... there.

But I walk past it every day. And it started whispering to me.

---

I think Anny is brave.

She paints the truth like she wants the whole world to see it.

I'm not like that.

I paint so the noise in my chest has somewhere to go.

I never show people what I make.

Not even Mama.

But lately… I feel something building.

A shape.

A silence that wants to take form.

---

So one night—when everyone was asleep—I went to the wall with a flashlight, a brush, and three jars of paint.

I didn't plan it.

I just started.

The first stroke was blue.

The second: gold.

Then gray.

Then a hand.

Then a doorway.

I didn't stop until dawn.

---

Over the next two weeks, I went back every night.

Sometimes for five minutes. Sometimes for hours.

I painted stories I've never said out loud.

The night Mama gave birth to the twins.
The time Papa let me fall asleep in his jacket after I had a panic attack.
The moment I saw Aris sitting in the garden, mouthing a word he didn't
know how to ask.
Anny painting fire with her eyes full of water.

And Mama—standing at the center of it all.

Not like a symbol.

Not like a saint.

But like a woman.

Tired. Alive. Still here.

No one saw it.

Until one morning, I woke up to find Mama standing in front of it, arms
crossed, not saying a word.

I froze in the doorway.

But she didn't turn.

She just said:

> "You saw all of us."

I nodded.

> "But you saw yourself too."

And that—somehow—broke me.

Because she was right.

CHAPTER THIRTY-EIGHT

# The Letter I Never Meant to Share
### (from Aris)

I never thought I'd write.

That was Anny's thing. Camille's. Mama's, always.

I was the one who observed. Who listened. Who watched things grow.

But something happened after she told us her story in the garden. After I saw Camille's wall. After I stood in front of Anny's painting and realized—

They weren't just telling her story.

They were telling ours.

And I hadn't said anything yet.

---

So I went to the kitchen late one night.

Everyone asleep.

I opened a notebook I kept hidden behind my school books. The one with drawings in the margins and half-sentences I was too afraid to finish.

And I wrote her a letter.

---

> Dear Maman,
I don't know why I'm writing this except that my chest feels heavy and I want to give you part of it so it doesn't feel so tight anymore.

I don't remember the country you left.
But I remember how you look at the sky sometimes like it's still holding a piece of you.

I remember when I found your notebook.

I remember not knowing what to do with your old name, like I was holding something sacred and dangerous at the same time.

I never told you that I started learning your language because I missed something I never even had.

And I still don't know how you did it—how you carried all of us across years and fear and silence without falling apart.

But you did.
And I see you now.

Not just as Maman.
But as someone who ran, who stayed, who rose, who forgave herself for surviving.

And I love you.

Not just because you're mine—
But because you made me brave without ever asking me to be.

Love,
Aris

---

I folded the page. Put it on her pillow.

I didn't wait for her to find it.

I just went to sleep.

But the next morning, when I walked into the kitchen, her arms were already around me before I could say a word.

## CHAPTER THIRTY-NINE

# The Answer
# Without Words
## (from Elara)

She didn't sleep after reading the letter.

Not because it hurt.

But because it was the most beautiful ache she had ever felt.

The paper had been folded in careful quarters. His handwriting—small, steady, upright—not slanted or loud, as if he wanted his words to be clear but never imposing.

It was the kind of writing that asked gently to be heard, not demanded it.

She read it once.

Then again.

Then once more, whispering each line like a prayer.

---

She didn't write back.

She didn't need to.

She waited until the house was still, then slipped into her studio and opened a blank canvas.

It had been a long time since she painted something without an audience in mind.

This wasn't for a gallery.

This wasn't for show.

This was for him.

---

It began with a small boy.

Seated at a table in the middle of a quiet storm.

Books open. A pen in one hand. His other hand reaching up—
not to shield himself,
but to hold the rain.

Around him, shadows leaned close. Not dark.
Just present.

And behind him—painted not with brilliance but with aching grace—
stood a woman.

Her shoulders wet.

Her hair swept back by wind.

She wore no crown.

She carried no sword.

But her wings unfolded behind her—
quiet, powerful, made of rain and light and memory.

She wasn't sheltering him.

She was standing with him.

Elara.

The mother.
The angel.
The storm-walker.

Not some distant saint—
but the one who had soaked herself in sorrow
so her child could walk forward without fear.

She didn't lift him.

She stood behind him—

silent, fierce, and absolutely unshakable.

An angel not above him—

but under the rain.

---

She painted through the night.

And in the morning, she left the canvas leaning against Aris's door.

No note.

Just the painting.

Titled in small letters along the bottom:

> "The Letter That Grew Wings."

## CHAPTER FORTY

# The House We Are Building
## (from all of them)

It started quietly.

No grand idea. No announcement.

Just a morning where Camille looked at the table, covered in sketches, letters, and brushes, and said:

> "We should keep this somewhere. All of it.
Not let it get lost."

He didn't look up when he said it. He didn't need to.

Anny stopped drawing.

Aris blinked, already writing something in his head.

Alexander whispered, "Like a book?"

"No," Camille said, softer now. "Bigger."

---

That summer, they climbed into the attic—the warmest room in the house, the dustiest, the one that smelled faintly of turpentine and old paper.

They didn't just collect.

They remembered.

They felt.

They sat in silence holding the letter Aris had written.

Touched the shoes their mother was given at sixteen.
Listened to old voice memos of Papa humming lullabies in kitchens across countries.
Read the notes Elara had never meant to share—scribbled in margins, stained with tears.

---

And then Anny brought up the biography Elara had written long ago:

> "The Hands That Planted Me: Stories of My Father."

Bound in soft blue linen.

Pages worn at the edges from Elara's fingers.

It told of a man who traveled oceans but always found his way back to her.
Who bled the same night she was born.
Who whispered "You are not alone" into her bones before she even knew what loneliness meant.

They placed it on the center shelf—

So even in death, he could be with them.

So the children could grow up knowing where her strength came from.

And that they carried it too.

---

They didn't speak much while they worked.

But they moved like people who understood the weight of what they were holding.

---

Anny framed her most sacred painting—The Woman and the Burning Field—and placed it next to one of Elara's earliest works.

Two flames.

Two voices.

One blood.

Camille painted the walls of the attic itself—each surface holding scenes:
Their mother as a girl.
Their father holding Elara's hand in a hospital chair.
A border. A storm.
A garden.
A newborn cry.

Aris wrote a poem titled "The Woman Who Stood in the Rain."
He tucked it inside the old notebook she once carried from city to city.

Alexander set up speakers in the corners of the attic, looping a single song he wrote—
"Not Even Silence Stays Empty."
It played softly, endlessly.

Like breath.

---

And Nan—their father—did what none of them expected.

He wrote a single letter.

Addressed to all of them.

> "I was trained to forget.
But I chose to remember—because your mother made remembering sacred.
I stayed because love made me brave.
You are the only truth I never had to question."

---

They named it The House We Are Building.

Not a book.

Not a gallery.

Not a monument.

Something alive.

Something warm.

A sacred room in the home that held everything they'd been given.

Not to show the world.

To never forget.

Everything she had carried.

---

Sometimes Elara came and stood in the doorway.

She wouldn't walk in.

She'd just rest her hand on the frame, close her eyes, and breathe and in that quiet, you could almost hear her heart say:

Not because she couldn't bear it.

But because she didn't need to step inside to know:

> "They saw me.
They heard me.

They became me—and more."

---

It wasn't just her survival they honored.

It was her love.

Her rain-soaked courage.

Her fire that never asked for glory.

And the silence she turned into light.

---

And in that attic, in that sacred space between memory and creation—beneath the paintings, the poems, the recordings, the letters, and her father's biography—every one of them could feel her whisper:

> "This... this is what I bled for.
This is why I stayed."

---

The End.

## CHAPTER FORTY

# The House We Are Building
## (from all of them)

It started quietly.

No grand idea. No announcement.

Just a morning where Camille looked at the table, covered in sketches, letters, and brushes, and said:

> "We should keep this somewhere. All of it.
> Not let it get lost."

He didn't look up when he said it. He didn't need to.

Anny stopped drawing.

Aris blinked, already writing something in his head.

Alexander whispered, "Like a book?"

"No," Camille said, softer now. "Bigger."

---

That summer, they climbed into the attic—the warmest room in the house, the dustiest, the one that smelled faintly of turpentine and old paper.

They didn't just collect.

They remembered.

They felt.

They sat in silence holding the letter Aris had written.

Touched the shoes their mother was given at sixteen.
Listened to old voice memos of Papa humming lullabies in kitchens across countries.
Read the notes Elara had never meant to share—scribbled in margins, stained with tears.

---

And then Anny brought up the biography Elara had written long ago:

> "The Hands That Planted Me: Stories of My Father."

Bound in soft blue linen.

Pages worn at the edges from Elara's fingers.

It told of a man who traveled oceans but always found his way back to her.
Who bled the same night she was born.
Who whispered "You are not alone" into her bones before she even knew what loneliness meant.

They placed it on the center shelf—

So even in death, he could be with them.

So the children could grow up knowing where her strength came from.

And that they carried it too.

---

They didn't speak much while they worked.

But they moved like people who understood the weight of what they were holding.

---

Anny framed her most sacred painting—The Woman and the Burning Field—and placed it next to one of Elara's earliest works.

Two flames.

Two voices.

One blood.

Camille painted the walls of the attic itself—each surface holding scenes:
Their mother as a girl.
Their father holding Elara's hand in a hospital chair.
A border. A storm.
A garden.
A newborn cry.

Aris wrote a poem titled "The Woman Who Stood in the Rain."
He tucked it inside the old notebook she once carried from city to city.

Alexander set up speakers in the corners of the attic, looping a single song he wrote—
"Not Even Silence Stays Empty."
It played softly, endlessly.

Like breath.

---

And Nan—their father—did what none of them expected.

He wrote a single letter.

Addressed to all of them.

> "I was trained to forget.
But I chose to remember—because your mother made remembering sacred.
I stayed because love made me brave.
You are the only truth I never had to question."

---

They named it The House We Are Building.

Not a book.

Not a gallery.

Not a monument.

Something alive.

Something warm.

A sacred room in the home that held everything they'd been given.

Not to show the world.

To never forget.

Everything she had carried.

---

Sometimes Elara came and stood in the doorway.

She wouldn't walk in.

She'd just rest her hand on the frame, close her eyes, and breathe and in that quiet, you could almost hear her heart say:

Not because she couldn't bear it.

But because she didn't need to step inside to know:

> "They saw me.
They heard me.

They became me—and more."

---

It wasn't just her survival they honored.

It was her love.

Her rain-soaked courage.

Her fire that never asked for glory.

And the silence she turned into light.

---

And in that attic, in that sacred space between memory and creation— beneath the paintings, the poems, the recordings, the letters, and her father's biography—every one of them could feel her whisper:

> "This... this is what I bled for.
This is why I stayed."

---

The End.

# The Sky She Painted
## (from Anny)

I was sixteen when I read the last page of her book.

Not the one she published.

The one she kept hidden, deep in the back of her drawer. The one none of us were supposed to find. Torn corners, pages full of her handwriting—the kind she only used when she thought no one was watching. There were places where the ink bled from tears. Places where she'd started a sentence and couldn't finish it.

Camille found the "key".

Of course he did.

We sat on the floor of her study, our backs against the bookcase. The twins were outside, chasing each other through the olive trees. Papa was asleep in his chair, his hand still curled like it used to when he held her fingers.

The light was soft. Dust danced in it.

And I turned the page.

And read.

And everything I thought I understood about my mother... came undone.

---

She had written everything.

About the mural they erased.
About the night she read a poem that got her followed.
About the time she ran barefoot down a border road with her name hidden in her sock.
About how she bled for me—almost died for me—before she ever heard me cry.

And about how terrified she was that we'd never know her.
Not really.

Not the parts she didn't show in the daylight.

Not the parts she buried beneath warm breakfasts and bedtime songs.

---

At the bottom of the last page, she had written this:

> "To Anny. To Camille. To Alexander and Aris.
You are my sky. You are the proof that I was here.
I hope one day you forgive the silences I kept.
I hope you feel the love I buried in every one."

---

I pressed my face to the page.

And cried like I was five again.

Because I remembered every morning she brushed my hair,
every moment she reached for me when I didn't know I needed her,
every time she said "I'm here" without needing to say anything else.

And I realized:

She had never hidden anything.

She had just carried it so I wouldn't have to.

---

People ask me what kind of mother she was.

And I tell them—

She was the kind who made safety feel sacred.
The kind who let love be fierce.
The kind who taught us that silence can be holy,
and survival can be art.

She didn't just raise us.

She shielded us with her own life.

She didn't just tell us to be strong.

She showed us what it looked like to be soft and still survive.

---

Camille paints now. So do I.

Sometimes we work side by side in her old studio.

The brushes feel like hers.
The colors still carry her breath.
And sometimes, when the light hits the canvas just right, I swear—
it's her hand guiding mine.

Papa says I have her eyes.
But I think what I really carry is her courage.

She gave it to all of us.

And she gave it without asking anything back.

---

The sky she painted?

It's still above us.

And we are still walking in her light.

---

# ACKNOWLEDGMENT

This book was not easy to write—

because it came from the softest and most bruised parts of memory.

It came from silence that once felt too dangerous to break.

It came from the fire of survival,

and the rain that followed.

To the ones who came before me—

who whispered strength into my bones even when I was too young to

understand it:

you live in every page.

To my father—

your absence still echoes.

But your love was a lighthouse, even from far away.

I carry your voice with me,

especially when mine trembles.

To the one who walked beside me through shadows,

held my hand through war, blood, and childbirth—

thank you for staying.

Thank you for choosing presence when silence would've been easier.

To my children—

you are my greatest act of courage.

Every story I buried was for your protection.
But this one—this one I wrote
so you would know me fully.
Not just as your mother.
But as the woman who bled, ran, fought, and rose
so you could be born in light.

You are my legacy.
You are the house I built when I had nothing left.
You are my reason.

And to you, reader—
thank you for stepping into this story gently.
Thank you for holding space for voices that were nearly erased.
For grief that took generations to soften.
And for love that outlived silence.

This book is a prayer.
A painting.
A memory.
A home.

And I give it to you
with nothing held back.

And truth—
even when quiet—
is never empty.

With all my heart,
Ellen Kapatou

# ACKNOWLEDGEMENT

To those who came before me—
who ran, who stayed, who carried their stories in silence—
this book is yours as much as mine.

To the voices that were nearly lost to history,
to the hands that created beauty in secret,
and to the mothers who survived so their children could breathe
freely—
thank you.

To my father, whose presence shaped my strength,
even in absence.
And to the man who walked beside me,
when walking was the hardest thing to do—
you were never just part of the story.
You were the reason I kept writing it.

To my children—
you are the light at the center of this house.
You are every brushstroke,
every note,
every word I couldn't say until now.

And to you, dear reader—

thank you for entering this space with tenderness.
For listening between the lines.
For choosing to remember, and to feel.

This story was not written for perfection.
It was written for truth.

And truth—
even when quiet—
is never empty.

With all my heart,
Ellen Kapatou